Teenage Wasteland: An American Love Story

Teenage Wasteland: An American Love Story

J. BRADLEY

WHISK(E)Y TIT
VT & NYC

Published in the United States by Whisk(e)y Tit: www.whiskeytit.com. If you wish to use or reproduce all or part of this book for any means, please let the author and publisher know. You're pretty much required to, legally.

ISBN 978-1-952600-03-6

Library of Congress Cataloguing in Progress

Cover design by Richard Buchanan.

First Whisk(e)y Tit paperback edition.

She doesn't remember what it's like to swim, the mermaid tells you after she finishes the first bottle of wine by herself. The mermaid says it's the only way she can feel underwater as she uncorks the second bottle. You're not sure if you should reach for her hand. You want to caress where you think her gills used to be. You think it's the neck but you didn't pay attention during sex ed about the biology of merpeople.

You cough up something oily and you've gotten used to this. You have always coughed up something oily for as long as you can remember. You ignore the burn in your throat, in your lungs. Your parents barely remember what it was like for them to breathe tolerable air, drink tolerable water. You barely remember what it was like to be human, your body a greenhouse of cancer, like all other non-mutated humans.

It is 9:03 PM. You try and get the mermaid's attention. You want to point out a star that you think you can see through the haze of still wheezing smoke stacks. You hope after she sees the star that she'll offer you at least a glass of wine. You like this mermaid. You hush the impatience on your tongue and in your hands.

You told everyone in second grade that you were really a mermaid. They believed you once you rolled up your pants and showed them your fused legs, the scaly psoriasis all over them. When your classmates asked what happened to your gills, you told them how your father took them away when you decided to live with your mother on land. When your classmates asked you what it was like to live underwater, you told them how your father took those memories away so you wouldn't need to miss him. Your best friend, the one with the melting face, hugged you and then everyone in class agreed that yes, you were really a mermaid.

Boys started paying attention to you more than the other girls who had two legs, or even one leg, under the full moon of their hormones. You discovered they were more interested in the mythology you made out of your body than who you were when their hands wandered during slow dances at school district sanctioned dating events. You slapped their hands away, warned them how her father would curse them.

You agreed to hang out with this boy, the one who coughed up oil, when he said he wanted to just talk and get to know you, when he promised to sit on his hands to prevent his impatience from getting to them. You steal two bottles of your mother's wine, tell the boy how the only way you can remember what it was like to feel underwater is by drinking the wine. The boy sits on his hands even after you polish off the first bottle, and open the second. The boy starts blurring. He takes his right hand out from beneath him, points at the sky, says, *look at the scar*, but you think that's impossible because there are no scars in the sky.

You watch as the guard feeds today's lesson into the VCR. The smell of gun oil from the guard's AK-47 reminds you to pay attention or else.

You try to focus on this installment of American history, how their version of the truth lost to the right version of truth as the American god intended, how the country is blessed to breathe in the holy spirit day in and day out. You cough up something oily in your hand, study the flecks of blood in the gob resting in your palm. The cock of the AK-47 tells you to look up and pay attention, or else.

You are grateful that the mermaid's last name starts with C and yours starts with M. You are close enough to map the beauty marks on the nape of her neck. You think about what her earlobes would taste like, whether her sweat is chemically equivalent to the pills you take to reduce how much oil and blood you cough up. The mermaid must feel your eyes because she turns her head to look at you. Just as your eyes meet, the guard fires a warning volley above your heads. Blood trickles from the fresh bullet holes in the ceiling and covers up how hard you're really blushing.

The guard feeds today's lesson into the VCR. It's the same one as yesterday as it was the day before. You know this when the orange-faced teacher in his American flag blazer appears on the screen. He pulls the pointer out of his blazer, extends it, and says let's begin in the way that conveys he's excited to teach you this lesson, as he was yesterday, as he was the day before yesterday.

You are used to seeing the same lesson over and over and over again. The state believes in the importance of repetition. You know better to question their facts after you watched your best friend, the girl with the melting face, almost lose her kneecap when she disagreed with the proctor of your science midterm.

You still feel underwater after last night, your mouth stuffed with wool, but it was worth it. The boy who coughs up oil maintained his composure. Even as he showed you the first star you've ever seen, he kept his hands and mouth to himself. You turn your head to look at him. Just as your eyes meet, the guard fires a warning volley above your heads. You watch the blood trickle from the bullet holes in the ceiling onto the boy's forehead and cheeks. You turn back to your lesson after the guard cocks the AK-47, again.

You hope the boy doesn't do anything stupid. The last boy who was into you, the one-armed one, rushed the proctor who shot your best friend. You thought it was romantic, even when he tried to say goodbye through the new hole in his throat, his vocabulary unable to clot. You used to think you were worth dying over until someone died on your behalf. You want to ask the boy who coughs up oil out, make the first move, to show him there is hope, to show him there is something worth living for, as intact as a boy who coughs up oil could be.

3

You take your shirt off in the bathroom and look at the scars riddling your torso. You thumb the one your father gave you after you fell from a desiccated tree outside of your house, how the bullet burned as it burrowed. You wanted to move your arms up and down to make angels from your blood in the dirt but you were too weak. The doctors discovered the greenhouse of cancer throughout your body after they removed the bullet and encased your leg in plaster. Your father kept what was left of the tree intact as a reminder of how it saved your life.

You wonder how the mermaid will react when she finally touches your skin, whether her hands would flinch at the scars until the right lie encourages her to teethe your neck. You know how the last boy she was into died and why. The mermaid forgets you were in the same testing room when the proctor shot her best friend, the girl with the melting face. You watched the boy rush the proctor, the bullet go through his throat, the mermaid cradling the dying boy as he tried to say goodbye, his blood where you wanted to be: all over her. You remember what the sex ed lesson said about the aphrodisiac of nobility: *heroism is the best way to begin a relationship.*

❧

You weren't surprised when the boy who coughs up oil stammered after you asked him if you could hang out again after history. You had to whisper so the guards wouldn't catch you asking him to see you outside of a school sanctioned dating event; any semblance of like or love is only allowed on their time, on their terms.

Your best friend, the girl with the melting face, asks you during lunch what makes the boy who coughs up oil worth your time. *He's the first boy who knows how to behave around you alone,* you say. *A yes is a key to a cage you might not want to open,* the girl with the melting face says. You look away when she takes a bite of her sandwich, covers her weeping cheeks to make sure the food doesn't escape. You're used to seeing things fall out of her face but you know how impolite it is to stare. *Where will you two go,* the girl with the melting face asks after she successfully swallows, and you shrug.

You haven't thought that far ahead. Even though you did the asking, you still expect him to tell where and how the way a man is supposed to tell you where and how. You remember how the sex ed tape told you how you can't trust a man that doesn't know how to plan, how to lead. You know you've already broken a rule by asking him to see you again, instead of him asking to see you again. Maybe you'll ask him to take you to the place you met last time, where he showed you your first star. Maybe you'll let him hold your hand if he can find another one.

4

You are worried how the mermaid's best friend, the girl with the melting face, will become an obstacle to winning the mermaid's heart, hand. You don't want to think of the girl with the melting face as a wall surrounding the mermaid but your pituitary gland pumps you full of venom, where the girl with the melting face becomes wider and higher, blackening what sunlight there is around the mermaid.

You cannot find anyone else in your grade or in the higher grades who would be interested wooing in the girl with the melting face. You are saddened by this, how no one is into the girl with the melting face, or at least is willing to admit their attraction to her. Someone somewhere swallows the shame of being into someone whose face perpetually melts, her skin drips, drips, drips.

You open to a blank page in your composition notebook, sketch the plans for a companion for the girl with the melting face. The graveyard a few miles away was recently flooded, the flood water pushing the coffins closer to the surface. You plan to go there, find bodies close to your age. You'll take down their names, locate their obituaries. You know how obituaries lie, how they place the departed on a pedestal impossible to climb. You may need to assemble the perfect boyfriend in piecemeal to make him perfect enough for the girl with the melting face to melt everywhere else, to wish upon a star she can make out through the clotted horizon to be with this perfect, yet piecemeal boy, to finally surrender to the tyranny of desire.

You worry about your best friend, the girl with the melting face. You see how loneliness spreads across her body like an infection when a new boy's name falls out of your mouth. You know your best friend, the girl with the melting face, wants you to come to your senses and ask her out instead. You both know that kind of love is against the law.

The history book you found half burnt in the basement of your house had pictures of boys holding boys, girls holding girls, the horizon covered in smiles and rainbow flags in mid-wave as they marched down the street. You showed the girl with the melting face the photos and she smiled, even though it hurts her the most to smile. She tried to hold your hand, but you pushed it away, not because you didn't want her to hold your hand, but because you were afraid of a bullet finding its way in through the basement window like a mosquito.

The TV reminds you what happens when who you love isn't sanctioned, the so-called guilty hanging above the open trap door like wind chimes, the mayor shouting over and over again the state-sanctioned equation, the state-sanctioned outcome. The TV won't shut off, no matter how hard you try. You know it never shuts off when they air these reminders. You are worried that your best friend, the girl with the melting face, may not survive the tyranny of her desire.

5

You shake yourself out of your daydream, the one where your hands run up the mermaid's back as you kiss her in the way that means *yes, yes, more, yes,* a second before the butt of a practice rifle cracks your jaw. You spiral to the floor, blood and oil flying out of your mouth, and onto the Sergeant's uniform. You cough up more blood and oil when the Sergeant slams the butt of his practice rifle into your stomach. He yells at the rest of the class about the dangers of not paying attention, how the enemy will chew you up and spit you out if your head isn't always on a swivel.

You don't know why you are required to be in this class. Your body is a greenhouse of cancer. Even though you continue to defy the odds, you always feel on the precipice of death. You tried to appeal to the principal about your uselessness on the front lines, and he waved you off, saying how useful you would be on the front lines as a human shield for someone healthy enough to fight against the state's enemies, how the foundation of patriotism consists of young men like yourself.

You think of the mermaid, her hand in yours, your mouths mingling, her hands running up and down your back as you both figure out the right name of the American god to use if anyone happens to be watching or listening. You pick yourself up off the ground, thank the Sergeant and ask him for another like you think a good soldier should.

❦

Your mother revises her story every time you ask her what happened to your father. He went from dying on the front lines to dying in a hospital bed to dying in a car accident to dying in a house fire to trampled to death during a food riot to executed for loving another man to leaving your mother for another woman to leaving you and your mother when your legs started fusing together to leaving you and your mother when psoriasis sprouted all over your fused legs like scales to leaving you and your mother when you basked under the full moon of puberty for the first time to leaving you and your mother to find something he lost, like his masculinity or patriotism, to prying the bear trap of family from his ankle. She always reminds you that it isn't your fault he left until she drowns in enough wine to moan how it is your fault he left her alone to die, to sleep in a half there bed where her hand wants to remember your father's shoulder or back but can't because it's been so long. You look at your wine wrecked mother and vow to never be her, sprawled out on a couch, weaving a constantly fluctuating history with waved hands, lit cigarette as needle and thread. She throws her (mostly) empty wine glass when you remind her that she isn't dying alone, that you'll always be there to watch, to be there and make sure her bones aren't picked over.

6

You map out the parts you needed from the obituaries: the track star's legs, the baseball player's arms, the weight lifter's torso, the choir boy's larynx, the swimmer's lungs, the boy scout's heart, the ROTC lieutenant's nerves, the linebacker's skeleton, the boxer's jaw, the goth boy's bottomless yearning, the shoulders of the fatherless boy who had three younger siblings to care for while his mother worked to keep a roof over their head, food in their bellies, clothing on their bodies. You plan on filling the missing parts with copper wire, batteries, whatever else you can think of that will operate this perfect boyfriend for the girl with the melting face, your piecemeal wingman clearing a path to the mermaid's open arms, open mouth.

One of your tumors questions the need for you to make a piecemeal wingman. *Why not just be the best boy you can be for her,* another tumor asks. *What does a tumor know about love,* you ask. Before they have a chance to answer, you swallow your daily pill to muzzle them. You say how it was a rhetorical question, that they know nothing of love. They only know how to blacken your organs, repeal, and replace them one by one. The bootleg music your parents gave you though would disagree; in the wrong hands, love is a cancer that no one survives one cell at a time. You listen to it over and over again and vow that your love will never be like that, and you'll prove that to the mermaid over and over again, once she gives you the chance.

❧

You never ask the boy who coughs up oil where the voices from inside his body come from, what they're saying when you're close enough to hear them. You're nice enough to ignore them, the same way you ignore the dribble of your best friend's skin and blood, the girl with the melting face.

The girl whose mouth opens sideways asks you if you're dating the boy who coughs up oil and you say maybe before it's too late to say no. You're not sure why you said maybe instead of no. You might like him or you might be claiming his body as your territory before the girl whose mouth opens sideways can. You notice after you say maybe how the girl's mouth curves like a waning, crescent moon.

The girl whose mouth opens sideways then tells you about how the boy who coughs up oil speaks throughout his body, and you nod as if you didn't already know this, didn't make out "you" and "beautiful" when you nuzzled up to the boy who coughed up oil as he showed you your first star through the wheezing smokestacks while you struggled for air from the second bottle of wine. You admired how the boy who coughs up oil still kept his hands and mouth to himself, even as his arms trembled as he moved side to side to keep his hands awake as he sat on them. Maybe, you might get to know the boy who coughs up oil enough to trust him, to listen to what his body says.

7

The boy who oozes promises to build a wall to a heaven that doesn't believe you belong there unless you have the right mutation and the right skin color. The boy who oozes has made this promise for every class election he's run in since sixth grade. Your class of eleventh graders was the first who believed him and elected him as class president. You rolled your eyes and coughed up more oil, less blood when his name was announced.

You didn't expect the boy who oozes to arm the hall monitors with collapsible batons. You hide as a pack of them descend on the boy who cries blood and beat him enough for his body to be a proper brick in the wall protecting a heaven from someone like you. *Why aren't you saving that boy*, one of your tumors ask. *The mermaid will love you for your courage.* You know you don't want your first kiss from her to be while you are dying in the mermaid's arms. You don't want her to taste your oil or your blood. You don't want your name added to the eulogy housed in her heart. You don't want to haunt her bedroom. The tumor hisses as it reads your thoughts. You feel the other tumors trying to compel your limbs to move, but you hush them. *You are already killing me*, you say. *There's no need to make my death come faster. Where will you go when I'm gone?*

❧

The boy who oozes eyes you everywhere you go. He slithers up to you, sucks his teeth as he inhales your scent, then asks if you'll be his first lady when he wins the election for student body president. The boy who oozes says you can choose your own charitable cause, as long as it makes him and his administration look good. You tell him first ladies are for real presidents and he glares at you. His slime trail boils as he slithers away. The boy who oozes throws a vow of how he'll show you what a real president looks like over your shoulder.

The boy who oozes slithers up to you after he wins the election. He gets close enough to pin you against a row of lockers. The boy who oozes sucks his teeth as he inhales your scent again, then asks if you'll be his first lady. He sweetens the offer by letting you choose who will be the first brick in the wall protecting a heaven that a girl like you belongs in when the American god finally asks her to come home. You would be the first mermaid to be a first lady, appealing to your sense of history. His chest squelches when you shove him away from you. You glare at the boy who oozes like you want to curse him and he slithers away, keeping his eyes on you to make sure you won't curse him. You can see in the way that the boy who oozes looks at you that he'll make you pay somehow for refusing to be by his side, caring for something he'll never care for, helping him build the wall to a heaven you belong in brick by brick.

8

You listen to the principal go on and on about the importance of dying for the state, whether on the front lines or to become a brick in the wall to heaven the new student body president wants to build to keep people like you out of it. He talks about a patchwork resilience darned by blood, how the youth of today ensures there will be a tomorrow.

You slip into a proposed memory of you and the mermaid having a picnic next to a lake that is somewhat safe to swim in. On the other side of the lake, the piecemeal wingman and the girl with the melting face have a picnic as well. The mermaid caresses your hand and thanks you for finding the girl with the melting face the perfect boyfriend. You are so hungry for each other, the picnic basket never gets opened.

One of your tumors tells you to wake up. You wake up and see the principal standing in front of you. You can smell the humid swamp of the principal as he drips on you. *Where were you,* he asks. You see his hands close into fists. You tell him how you were thinking about the best way for your body to serve the state, how you want to incubate bullets so the youth of tomorrow will caress your name etched on a wall and thank you for your service. The principal pauses. He opens his right hand and puts it on your shoulder. The principal calls you a good example that everyone else in this assembly should follow. You melt in your chair and hope the mermaid wasn't here to see this.

❧

You heard from the girl whose mouth opens sideways that the boy who coughs up oil said he wanted his body to serve the state, to incubate bullets so the youth of tomorrow could caress his name etched on a wall and thank him for his service. Part of you feels disappointed that the boy who coughs up oil would put the needs of the state over your blossoming need for him. Part of you though doesn't trust the girl whose mouth opens sideways. You've seen the way she eyes the boy who coughs up oil. It's the same way the boy who oozes eyes you as you hop down the hallway. It's the same way the boy who oozes eyes you when you dissect the corpses of animals to better learn their biology. You could ask the boy who coughs up oil his side of the story but you know he might not tell you the whole truth if the truth loses you; boys never tell the girls the truth unless the truth involves boys telling girls how they really feel.

The girl with the melting face confirms, yes, the boy who coughs up oil said he wanted his body to serve the state, to incubate bullets so the youth of tomorrow could caress his name etched on a wall and thank him for his service. The girl with the melting face also confirms why the boy who coughs up oil said these things: the principal stopped the assembly and stood in front of the boy who coughs up oil when the principal caught him not paying attention. The last time a student didn't pay attention to the principal during an assembly, the principal made everyone watch as he buried the student in the swamp of his body.

9

You cannot find limbs not gnawed by animal or decay as you gather the parts you need to start construction on your piecemeal wingman, the perfect boyfriend to distract the girl with the melting face so you and the mermaid can get to know each other enough to turn any place you both want into a dark corner to feast on each other. Your parents ask you what that smell is coming from the basement and you tell them it's your science project for the district science fair coming up in a month. They ask if they can come down to look at it and you tell them no, you don't like anyone looking at a work in progress. They ask you to do something about the smell then, and the growing number of insects swarming around the house. You tell them the insects are part of the project and they roll their eyes and walk away.

You are having a hard time staying up in classes since you are up all night digging and extracting parts and pieces for the girl with the melting face's perfect boyfriend. There is more blood than oil in your phlegm since you've asked the tumors to help keep you awake, to operate your body as if you're awake when your eyelids droop. *Don't do anything I wouldn't do*, you tell them, and you're not sure if they'll do anything you wouldn't do. They know they need your body to keep them alive but they don't need you necessarily intact to keep them alive. You're afraid this might be what finally lets the tumors overthrow your control of your body but the mermaid's love is worth the risk.

♪

After the girl with the meting face drinks half a bottle of wine you stole from your mother's cupboard, she lets out the rumor that the boy who coughs up oil is robbing graves. You ask her where the rumor came from, and she said it came from the boy who oozes and the girl whose mouth opens sideways, and they said they heard the rumor from the boy with no skeleton. They all had different reasons why the boy who coughs up oil might be doing this. The boy with no skeleton says the boy who coughs up oil is running out of time and is looking for replacement body parts. The girl whose mouth opens sideways says the boy who coughs up oil is putting together a pretend mermaid to practice with so he will be ready when the real mermaid finally says *yes, yes, yes*. The boy who oozes says the boy who coughs up oil is putting together a perfect boyfriend for himself to hold hands with. Everyone knows though the boy who oozes has it out for the boy who coughs up oil because of you.

You and the girl with the melting face sneak out of your house. You follow the boy who coughs up oil as he leaves his house, shovel perched on his shoulder. You watch him enter the graveyard, break hallowed ground. *Maybe it's the wine making us see these things*, you tell the girl with the melting face. You and the girl with the melting face stagger away, the wool starting to expand in your mouths. You wonder what the boy who coughs up oil is up to, whether he'll tell you the truth instead of what you want to hear.

IO

You wake up to your hand clutching a pen. You look down at your desk, notice a sheet of notebook paper filled with scrawl, probably from one or more of your tumors. You read the letter and one or more of your tumors has declared their love for the girl whose mouth opens sideways. The one or more tumors that love her try to stop you from crumpling the letter and throwing it away. You feel them tugging your muscle and nerves, saying *no don't* over and over again. You cough up something oily and bloody on the letter, smear the glob of phlegm all over it. The tumors stop tugging your muscles and nerves. The one or more tumors that love her vow revenge, vow their hands in hers, vow to abandon you for her the first chance that they get.

You look at the half complete piecemeal wingman. You don't know how much longer you can let your tumors pilot your body when you fall asleep in class. You cannot trust your body around the mermaid when you are alone with her, which is why you sit on your hands and bite your tongue when you are alone with her. You now fear the impeachment of your body, the tumors shedding the idea of you until the idea of you is dust in a carpet waiting to be inhaled and coughed. You know though that you have to finish the piecemeal wingman in order to be alone with the mermaid, encourage the fury beneath your bodies to ravage, ravage, ravage each other.

❧

You notice the boy who coughs up oil walking like one of those zombies still roaming in the city formerly known as Atlanta that the news shows from time to time to remind new moms and dads the perils of vaccinating their children. You risk being seen by everyone when you and your best friend, the girl with the melting face, sit with him during lunch and you ask him what's going on, what's up, as if you two didn't see him shamble into a graveyard after midnight, shovel perched on his shoulder. The boy who coughs up oil looks up at you in a way you don't recognize and says in a voice you don't recognize he's been up late working on his science project. You ask him what's his science project and he says it's a secret, how all will be revealed at the district science fair. You see the girl with the melting face wants to tell the truth but you put your hand over her mouth. Where are your manners, you say to her, and the girl with the melting face gives you a look that tells you to make him tell you the truth. A hall monitor walks over, extends his baton with the flick of a wrist, and asks the three of you if there's a problem. You look up, into the hall monitor's eyes, and say that you didn't want your best friend to spill a secret. *A good person doesn't have secrets*, the cafetorium monitor says. *No one here is a good person then, I guess*, you reply, looking at him like you know a secret he's hiding. The hall monitor smashes the lunch tray in front of the boy who coughs up oil, storms away. You watch the boy who coughs up oil wake up. He asks what you two are doing here. The lunch bell rings before you two can answer.

II

You meet the mermaid in the same place you met her for your first date: the abandoned auto factory where the fathers without jobs go when they leave their houses to go to work to continue the illusion of winning bread and gathering bacon. You got here early to sweep away the empty beer bottles, clear a place for you and the mermaid to sit and talk, sit and look at each other, sit and maybe become a tangle of limbs and spit.

When the mermaid shows up, you notice her lack of a wine bottle. You notice the lack of eye shadow on her eyelids, the lack of eyeliner around her eyes. You notice there's no lipstick smeared around her mouth. You think she trusts you enough to look at her as she actually is beneath the makeup, her way of testing whether you would be into her as she appears naturally. All that hope goes away when she crosses her arms and asks if you're ok, what you've been up to. You stammer out how you've been up late working on your science project, how you haven't been sleeping well because of how driven you are to win the district science fair. She asks whether it's you or one or more of your tumors who's really talking to her right now. You say it's you talking, not one or more of your tumors, and the mermaid keeps her arms crossed, furrows her brow to try and break you.

❧

You are more disappointed than angry when the boy who coughs up oil told you to meet him at the abandoned auto factory, where you and him had your first date. You thought he would meet you somewhere different, like by the lake that's somewhat safe to swim in, or the mall where the only store open is a Sears, the rest of the mall overtaken by the gangrenous economy. The mall would have been especially perfect as you two could have snuck past the guards, found the perfect, empty store to continue getting to know one another.

You decide if he's not going to try and be romantic, won't try to be daring and different, won't try to do something new, that he wasn't worth the effort to put on your best face, make your mouth the promise of a feast. You decide if he's not going to try and be romantic, won't try to be daring and different, won't try to do something new, then you'll ask him what he's trying to find in his late night visits to the graveyard. You decide if he's not going to be romantic, not try to be daring and different, not try to do something new, then you won't steal a bottle or two of your mother's wine to bring with you, keep yourself landlocked.

You walk through the doorway of the abandoned auto factory and see the boy who coughs up oil tidying up where you two will sit. You bury a smile before it has a chance to curl your lips. You cross your arms and clear your throat, and the boy who coughs up oil looks at you the way you want a boy to look at you when he's in like or in love. You don't wait for him to say something before you dive in with your questions: *Are you ok? What are you up to?* You're not sure if it's one of his tumors talking through him, so you ask him whether he's talking to you or one of his tumors. When he freezes and stammers, you furrow your brow, hoping your disappointment will finally get him to do something unboylike and tell you the truth.

12

You can't get out of your head how you just stood there as the mermaid interrogated you about how you were and what you were up to, and you couldn't (or wouldn't) tell her anything. You weren't sure how she would react if you told her that your science project isn't for the district science fair but to make a perfect piecemeal wingman to distract the mermaid's best friend, the girl with the melting face, so you and the mermaid could be more alone and wallow in and around each other's like or (maybe, hopefully, someday) love.

One of your tumors makes fun of you for your inability to be anything but a teenaged boy, one who would rather hide or lie than be who they really are. Another tumor shows you a portrait they've made of the girl whose mouth opens sideways from bits and pieces of your frayed circulatory system. You remind the tumors how the mermaid is the one you want and you feel the tumors on your lungs chuckle. You find your pills, take one to muzzle the tumors.

You can't get out of your head how the mermaid looked at you before you walked away. The disappointment in her eyes slit you open. You put in The Cure's *Disintegration* and let the ache metastasize throughout your soul. You always listen to this album when you feel like you've failed at love as you have many times over throughout middle school and high school. You pray for your arms to be an umbrella to pull the mermaid close as it rains.

❧

The cork disintegrates as you open the bottle of wine you stole from your mother. Your mother doesn't notice or doesn't care that you steal her wine as she is always underwater. When she does surface long enough to breathe, you're not sure what version of her will speak to you: the mother who loves you, the mother who regrets having you, the mother who blames you for your father, her husband walking out on her, the mother who doesn't care what you do as long as you don't cost her money, the mother who just wants to keep swimming until she falls asleep on the couch bathing in the glow of the TV.

You understand why your best friend, the girl with the melting face, doesn't like boys the way you do: their hands and mouths and tongues have a shallow courage. You're disappointed that the boy who coughs up oil didn't tell you the truth, let alone anything, but you're not surprised. You typically like older boys because they've started to grow out of the need to not tell the truth when the truth could hurt how you look at them, though you've had to prod and pry from time to time.

You stare at the cork particles swimming through your wine as you swirl it around and around your wine glass to aerate it enough where you can take a sip without flinching. You ask yourself how many more chances will you give the boy who coughs up with oil to tell the truth. You stop swirling your wine and sip, start to dive.

13

The right eye of your piecemeal wingman stares you down as you straighten his cheek on the mannequin's skull. You need to keep the piecemeal wingman's skin supple enough to stretch across the wire skeleton you've going to pay the boy without a jaw to build for you limb by limb during his shop class.

You think of seeing the mermaid cozying up to the class president, the boy who oozes. You think of the way she looks at him, and then looks at you that says *this should be your arm, your words that I should be hanging on, not his.* You know she's punishing you for not telling her the truth about what you've been up to, your gathering and building of the piecemeal wingman who will steal the heart of the girl with the melting face, the mermaid's best friend.

You couldn't stop staring at the boy without a jaw's flopping and flailing tongue as he writes down his price for building you the wire skeleton needed for your piecemeal wingman: a new jaw. You ask him why he couldn't just build one for himself during shop class and he writes how he wants what every boy wants: to feel a girl's fingertips coaxing sighs from his jaw, coaxing his lips to meet her lips. The boy without a jaw wouldn't be able to feel that if he made himself a jaw from sheet metal, gun metal, or wood. You promise him to find him the right jaw, but not the perfect one. The perfect jaw is reserved for the piecemeal wingman who (you hope) will woo the girl with the melting face with his piecemeal perfection.

❧

Your stomach curdles at the sight of the boy who oozes, and it takes every ounce of your will to swallow the rising tide of bile and vomit when you ask the boy who oozes how you can help make your school great again. When the boy who coughs up oil stumbles upon the two of you talking, you grab his arm, hang on every word. You glance at the boy who coughs up oil. You know the boy who coughs up oil gets the message when you see him wince at the sight of the two of you together, at the sight of you fawning over the boy who oozes. You think about your biology test coming up in the sixth period as the boy who oozes blah blah blah blahs about building the wall to a heaven to keep a girl like you safe brick by brick, body by body.

The muck of the boy who oozes won't come off even after you wash your hands four times. You drown your hands in perfume to mask the smell of the muck sticking to your hands. You wish his skin oozed more like a film so you could just pinch it and peel it away little by little until your hands smell like you. You look in the mirror. You hope the boy who coughs up oil is rattled enough to finally tell you what's going on with him, what he's up to, why he's visiting graveyards late at night. You don't know if you can stomach the boy who oozes again, but you're willing to do what it takes to get the truth.

14

One of your tumors, probably the one that's in love with the girl whose mouth opens sideways, reminds you while you sleep of that time in fifth grade when your class stared at you after you spelled freedom f-r-e-e-d-o-m during your class's qualifier to see who would compete in the Jefferson Beauregard Sessions the Third's Elementary's spelling bee finals (Go Marauders!). One of your classmates, the girl with the weeping hole on her chest, said *no, that's not how you spell freedom, you spell freedom g-l-o-c-k*. Another classmate, the boy who had hands for feet, said *no, you spell freedom g-o-d*. Another classmate, the girl with no arms or legs said *no, you spell freedom n-u-c-l-e-a-r-h-o-l-o-c-a-u-s-t*. All of your other classmates just stared, just stared as your teacher walked over, raised your arm, and declared you the winner. Your classmates kept staring even after the spelling bee was over.

When you wake up, you ask the tumor, the one probably that's in love with the girl whose mouth opens sideways, why did it remind you of the first and last time you spelled a word based on the dictionary's interpretation instead of its appropriate patriotic interpretation, and it brings up the classroom again, the classmates sitting and staring. It pans the memory to the girl whose mouth opens sideways looking at you with longing, hands propping up her chin, Cupid arrow drunk on your rebellion. You tell the tumor that your heart spells like (maybe, maybe, maybe love, one day, if you are patient, patient and lucky) as m-e-r-m-a-i-d.

➤

The girl whose mouth opens sideways eyes you as you talk to the boy who oozes. You can feel her squinting at you as you clear away the mucky bangs from the boy who oozes's eyes, straighten his collar. The girl whose mouth opens sideways waits until the boy who oozes walks away before walking up to you, her lips curled like a waning moon. She says: *a boy's heart doesn't belong in a jar that you can break open in case of emergency, like when you're in danger of being alone at a school sanctioned dating event like Homecoming or Prom.* The girl whose mouth opens sideways slaps you across the face so hard, everyone stops and stares at the both of you, as if time is suspended.

You ball your hands into fists and think of your options. You could hit the girl whose mouth opens sideways until you straighten her waning mouth into a flat, vertical line, until her teeth bend and snap off, until there's blood coming out of her mouth, spilling onto the floor, and your hands. You could hit the girl whose mouth opens sideways in her stomach, until you can see what she had for lunch, maybe even breakfast. You keep your fists clenched, to your side. You know you might get called into the principal's office, get scolded for not following one of the most important rules in the school's code of conduct: peace through strength, but you know a better way to hurt her. You grab her shoulder, pull yourself close enough only she can hear this: *he will never love you, he will never be yours.* You walk away as if nothing happened, resist looking over your shoulder.

15

You dream of a future where you and the mermaid are in your twenties, you're still alive despite the tumors, despite the bullets you've taken for healthier men on the front lines during whatever war was the trendiest or the noblest. You look out the window and see that the wall to a heaven someone like you doesn't belong in remains unfinished, the bricks and bodies chipped away by weather, birds, and time. You hear the boy who oozes, who is now the president who oozes, on TV in the background yelling about the need to keep building the wall to a heaven keeping someone like out of it, the age limit lowered to who could be president when the survival rate past the age of forty became impossible. You've trained yourself to ignore the TV when he speaks as the TV doesn't allow you to shut off (by law) when the president speaks or spews. You hear the door open, and you turn and face the mermaid who holds your daughter in her arms. She has her mother's tail and fin, your oily cough. The tumors remove the floor out from beneath the mermaid, and your daughter and you watch them fall. When you try to run to the hole, the tumors build a wall around the hole. You beat your fists against the bricks, crying and yelling. You wake up in a cold sweat, standing in front of your piecemeal wingman. You lower the baseball bat you don't remember carrying and stare at the piecemeal wingman's dried blood all over it.

You are surprised when you dream of a version of yourself with two actual legs working with your arms to splash around in the ocean. You are often underwater from the bottle or bottles of wine you stole from your mother, and that kind of drowning doesn't let you remember your dream. You splash around an ocean not filled with bobbing carcasses, like an ocean the teacher on one of the earth science VHS tapes described, safe and blue. You make it back to shore just before the ache in your arms and legs sets in. You stretch and bask in the sun that feels warm, but not scalding, the ozone layer still strong enough to reduce the sting of the sun on your skin. You scrunch sand between your toes and then look around at the beach. You stop scrunching when you see dead boy after dead boy after dead boy in the sand, riddled with bullets, seagulls pecking at the bodies. You gag at the smell of the sun-warmed bodies. You feel a hand on your shoulder and turn to see the boy who oozes smiling his mudhole smile, bearing his poison teeth. *I did this for you*, he says, pointing at the sun-warmed bodies strewn about the beach. *You deserve the best wall to protect a heaven you and I belong in. Don't worry, there are more boys coming who will help build the wall brick by brick, and will become bricks when they are spent and useless. You won't have to dirty your pretty, precious hands.* You wake up in a cold sweat, the psoriasis running up and down your fused legs burning.

16

You stare at the blank sheet of notebook paper on your desk. You sharpen a pencil, twiddle it, chew on it, twiddle it, stop. You hover the pencil over the page, your brain trying to send signals to your right hand, but your right hand tells your brain what it wants to do is a bad idea. Your brain disagrees with your right hand, but you start to think maybe it's not your right hand telling your brain this is a bad idea, but the tumor that's probably in love with the girl whose mouth opens sideways telling your right hand to tell your brain this is a bad idea. You remind your right hand that you are the captain of this body and your right hand responds by snapping the pencil in half. You find your pills and your right hand goes slack when you try opening the pill bottle so you use your mouth instead. While the pill bottle cap is between your teeth, your right hand tries snatching the bottle out of your left hand and you spill the pills on your desk, spit the pill bottle cap out, and take a pill like a bird pecking at seed. After a few minutes, your right hand behaves again. You scoop the pills back into the pill bottle. You find the pill bottle cap and seal the pill bottle. You dig through a drawer to find another pencil, sharpen it. You twiddle and chew, twiddle and chew, twiddle and chew as the words come to you, the words to explain to the mermaid a revised version of events going on, a better version of you.

❧

A folded slip of paper falls out of your locker and in front of your best friend's feet, the girl with the melting face. You crouch down and snatch it from the floor before the girl with the melting face has a chance to react. You feel her skin drip on your bare shoulders as she keeps looking over them, asking *who's it from? who's it from? who's it from?*

You drop the slip of paper in your open purse, zip it shut, and your best friend sighs. The warning bell saves you from further interrogation.

You have a hard time focusing on today's math lesson. You lose yourself in the question of who wrote the note, what's written on it. Is the author the boy who oozes, the boy who coughs up oil, the girl with the melting face, the girl whose mouth opens sideways, or a new suitor or new enemy who has declared war against your heart, your desire. The woman on TV talks about the Pythagorean theorem and a couple of the boys around you laugh, and high five after one of them says that you could be the "a" to their "b" and "c". You get up and slap the one who said that across the face. He touches his mouth, looks at the blood on his fingers. The boy cocks back his fist, and you hear the guard pull back and release the charging handle of his AK-47. The boy sits down before the guard has a chance to aim and fire. The guard lowers his AK as you and the rest of the class return to today's lesson.

17

You sit by the phone and wait for the mermaid's call. You should be thinking about how to repair and rebuild the piecemeal wingman in the basement, but you're afraid if you keep going with building the piecemeal wingman from perfect boy parts to get the girl with the melting face to fall in love with him so you and the mermaid can be alone more often, one of your tumors, the one probably in love with the girl whose mouth opens sideways, can hijack your body and express its love for her through your arms and your mouth, destroying all hope and possibility you have of being with the mermaid for the rest of your (short) life. You took a double dose of your pills to keep your tumors quiet while you wait for the mermaid to call. She needs to hear from you how you feel about her, about how to solve this equation of you and her to equal we, not your tumors.

You think about the letter you wrote. You think about whether the mermaid was the only one who read it. You think about whether anyone else wrote the letter, and if they did, would they carve a target on your back since you demonstrated feelings, and it's against the law of this teenage wasteland for boys to express their feelings through the written word, how the right way to express your feelings to the one you want is through action, your hands and mouth as your tools.

❥

You take the folded slip of paper out of your purse and put it on your desk and stare at it like it's a time bomb waiting for you to defuse it, the time bomb that could shake the foundations of your heart, you sifting through the rubble for reason, a name to cry out in the dusk of your feelings. You uncork tonight's bottle of wine (carefully), pour some in a coffee mug, and sip. You wait until you've reached the right depth to unfold the slip of paper and smooth it out. You can see from the salutation, the "dear beloved mermaid" above the first line of the unfolded notebook paper that the author of this letter is the boy who coughs up oil. You've seen his handwriting before, but only the block letter version of it. The boy who coughs up oil is the only boy you know who would be brave or foolish enough to use words like "beloved" when it comes to describing how he feels about you; it's one of the many reasons you like him. Yet, you stare at the "dear beloved mermaid" salutation and question whether you should continue reading. You can't tell when a letter lies to you. You can't look in a letter's eyes to dig beneath an answer for the body beneath it. A letter can only tell you what's been written in it, maybe leave a paper cut or two on your fingertips if you don't handle the paper properly. You take a deep breath, pick up the coffee mug, and spill a little bit of wine on the letter to smear the ink. You'll tell the boy who coughs up oil how you got his letter, but you spilled wine on it, and you'll produce the letter to show him you're not lying. You'll ask him as he stares at the ruined carcass of his letter, what was on it, what he wanted to say, and wait for his reply.

18

You look at the calendar hanging inside your locker, at the days you've crossed out and note that it has been five days since you dropped the letter in the mermaid's locker, five days and she has not called, not walked up to you, not said anything other than *hi* or nodded her head when you passed by her in the hall, not said anything when you asked her to pick up the pencil or pen you dropped in class other than you're welcome when you thanked her for picking up your pencil or pen you dropped. One of your tumors says she never got the letter. Another one of your tumors, the one that probably is in love with the girl whose mouth opens sideways, says she got the letter and doesn't like you anymore, how she's built a wall around the heaven that is her heart to keep boys like you out of it, boys who would rather tell girls how much they like them instead of show them through action, with hand and mouth as the tool. Time starts slowing, and you know the mermaid is near because time starts slowing as she walks closer and closer to where you're standing and staring at the days you marked on your calendar to show how long it has been since you dropped the letter in the mermaid's locker. Your tumors say *no, don't. No, don't do this, don't risk the execution of your heart in the public square of this hallway, of this high school*, and you don't listen to them as you close your locker, step in front of the mermaid, and ask whether she got that thing you sent her.

❧

You watch the boy who coughs up oil emerge from the chrysalis of his locker and stand in front of you and your best friend, the girl with the melting face. *Hi*, he says, *did you get that thing I sent you?* The girl with the melting face looks at you, then looks at him, then looks at you. Everyone else in the hall stops, looks at him, looks at you. You and him, the boy who coughs up oil, know that you hold his heart in your hand at this moment, and you could use his own heart to gut him or use it as an invitation to invite him to the heaven of your arms. In the corner of your eye, you see the guards, the ones devoted to promoting and protecting chastity outside of school sanctioned dating events, looking at you, then at the boy who coughs up oil, then back at you. You think how brave or how dumb the boy who coughs up oil is, how he is willing to risk a bullet to hold your hand, maybe hold more of you if he is patient and you are willing to trust your body to his touch. *Yes, you say, yes, I got your note about the pop quiz that might be coming up in our history class tomorrow. I don't know how I missed that.* You watch the boy who coughs up oil look around and notice the guards, the ones who protect and promote chastity looking at them, and he says *good*, and walks past you and your best friend, the girl with the melting face. The warning bell rings and everyone scatters.

19

You look at the beaten piecemeal wingman, at the obituaries you gathered to create your blueprint for the piecemeal wingman, the one that the girl with the melting face would fall in love with so you and the mermaid can get lost in each other's eyes, hands, legs, and mouths: the track star's legs, the baseball player's arms, the weight lifter's torso, the choir boy's larynx, the swimmer's lungs, the boy scout's heart, the ROTC lieutenant's nerves, the linebacker's skeleton, the boxer's jaw, the goth boy's bottomless yearning, the shoulders of the fatherless boy who had three younger siblings to care for while his mother worked to keep a roof over their head, food in their bellies, clothing on their bodies. You look at the beaten piecemeal wingman, wonder whether he needs all of these perfect parts from these perfect boys to be the perfect boy for the girl with the melting face to fall in love with. Maybe, he just needs the right brain, the right tongue to weave a wooing spell around the waist of the girl with the melting face.

Why do you keep doing this, one of your tumors asks. *You should be man enough to win the mermaid on your own, without a wingman to distract her best friend. The mermaid needs a man, not a boy.* You ask the tumor if it knows what it's like to be a boy, how daunting it is to be direct and courageous, how convolution is the clearest path to love. You cough up something oily into your hand. You look at the fluid in your palm and the flecks of blood are trying to spell "don't" but you ignore the n, the apostrophe, and the t.

❧

You have not spoken to the boy who coughs up oil since his attempt to confront you in the hallway outside of his locker in front of others, in front of the guards who protect and enforce chastity outside of school sanctioned dating events, in front of your best friend, the girl with the melting face. You are giving the boy who coughs up oil time to think, time to reflect on how he can best approach you without taking a bullet. You've seen too many boys want to take a bullet for you, thinking they could woo you with a survivable exit wound.

You keep having that dream where you emerge from the ocean with two actual legs, where you see dead boy after dead boy in the sand and the boy who oozes smiling his mud hole smile, bearing his poison teeth saying how he did this for you, pointing at the sun-warmed bodies strewn about the beach and you wonder whether you should convince the boy who oozes the wall to heaven he wants to build is a good idea, stomach hanging on his arm to quell the lust for blood in the hall monitors' batons, stomach risking losing the boy who coughs up oil forever to save boys and girls like him from becoming bricks in the wall to a heaven girls like you belong in. You look out the window, at stars you cannot see through the smoke-choked sky, and you laugh at the notion of such a thing as "forever". Forever is how you were born with fused legs riddled with psoriasis, how the boy who coughs up oil has tumors that talk to him, and never to you.

20

You wake up in the nurse's office. You start to get up but the leather straps cinched around your wrists won't let you. You look at the blood and bruises on your knuckles and ask yourself what happened. *They were coming for you*, one of your tumors says. You ask *who*, and the tumor says, *shut your eyes and remember*. You watch on the movie screen of your eyelids how four hall monitors descend upon you like a swarm with their batons, yelling how you have been selected to be the next brick in the wall to a heaven that keeps people like you out of it. You block the first two or three baton strikes with your forearm. The fourth one causes something in you to snap. You watch your fist burrow into a hall monitor's stomach, expelling the air out of him with a loud oomph. Your right elbow breaks the jaw of the hall monitor behind you. You lift another hall monitor and throw him into a row of lockers. The last hall monitor, the one still standing, drops his baton and runs. You turn your attention to the hall monitor on the floor, trying to catch his breath, and you kick him in the stomach so hard, he flips over on his back. You mount the hall monitor and punch his face over and over again until two guards lift you off of him and drag you away. *What did I do*, you ask. *The right thing*, another tumor says.

❧

When you don't see the boy who coughs up oil in your American History class, you ask around to find out where he is. You saw him earlier during your lunch period, eating alone as he usually does. One boy, the one who lost his left arm to the swamp of the principal's body, said that the hall monitors took the boy who coughed up oil for reeducation. One girl, the one with eyes in her cheeks, her eye sockets swollen shut, says the hall monitors turned the boy into a brick for the wall to heaven that the class president, the boy who oozes, wants to build to protect girls like you and keep boys like the boy who coughs up oil out of it. The girl whose mouth opens sideways says: *everything you've heard isn't true. There were four hall monitors who came at him, waving batons, yelling how the boy who coughs up oil was selected to be the next brick in the wall around heaven. The boy who coughs up oil stood there and took two or three shots from the batons before fighting back. All but one of the hall monitors managed to escape.* Escape, you ask. Yes, escape. The girl whose mouth opens sideways points out the row of lockers with a boy sized dent in them. *He threw one of the monitors here. The one who didn't escape* (the girl whose mouth opens sideways pauses, her eyes water.) *The boy who coughs up oil beat a hall monitor to death. He* (the girl whose mouth opens sideways starts crying) *beat one of the hall monitor's faces in. I watched* (the girl whose mouth opens sideways breaks the conversation off and runs away, crying). You know you need to speak to the boy who oozes before he retaliates, before this escalates into a full scale war.

21

Everyone in the hallway makes room for you as you limp to your locker. They stare and stare and stare like they have never stared at you before. Your right hand still aches from the hall monitor's face and you struggle to open the combination lock. You look around and see everyone still looking at you.

You couldn't believe it when the principal said no charges would be filed. He beamed over how you followed the school code of conduct regarding conflict: peace through strength. The principal didn't know you had it in you and had to watch the security footage three times to confirm that you, the boy who coughs up oil, fought off two hall monitors, and killed one. Not just killed, destroyed. *We need more boys like you at this school*, he said. *Boys who are willing to make the weak bleed.*

You see the boy who oozes and five hall monitors approach you. You see their batons are still holstered, how the boy who oozes is the nucleus of this cell of violence. The cell stops in front of you. *Want us to handle this,* your tumors ask, and you say *not yet.* The boy who oozes vows that you will be a brick in the wall to heaven he wants to build to keep boys like you out of it, no matter how many hall monitors it takes. *If I kill enough of them, they might kill you for me*, your tumors say through your mouth.

❧

Beneath the full moon of your hormones, you would tear off the boy who coughs up oil's clothes with your teeth. You would lick the blood of his enemies off his skin and kiss him with your mouth full of the blood of his enemies, you and him entwined as a throbbing tombstone marking the defeat of his enemies, now your enemies because they were his enemies. You would want to dig your nails and your teeth into his skin, scar him with your love, make him bleed with your love so you can taste him on those nights you're alone and he's killing his enemies, who become your enemies, and you would count the days until he comes home from the latest war, and you would count the days until you are both saying *yes* so loud it would break through the wall now surrounding heaven.

Your brain, though, pulls you away from the full moon of your hormones, reminds you that you like the boy who coughs up oil because he did not lust for blood and death, like all of the other boys in school, that the boy who coughs up oil was allergic to things like bravery and bullets, and you like him for that, for the brain he wants to use, the softness of his heart, the romantic in the coffin of his body, not the body count he wants to rack up some day.

22

You can't remember when you have never been at war with your own body. Your parents sold themselves off bit by bit, piece by piece, to give you what you need to keep fighting until they finally got jobs where they didn't have to sell themselves off bit by bit, piece by piece. When you had friends once, they would ask why your dad only has one eye, a hand missing three fingers, why your mom only has one leg, why she always wears long sleeve shirts in this perpetual summer, and you told them they lost them in a war fighting for freedoms that let us keep breathing the America god's exhale. They stopped being your friends once they caught you coughing up something oily for the first time, as if you could pass on your tumors through blood and spit and skin, your defective body infecting them with your defectiveness. You forgot though how the tumors feeding from your body saved you that day when your "friends" discovered your defect and tried to kill you, tried to bury you alive in the sandbox adjacent to the playground. The tumors did what you could not do. They guided your hand into one of your friend's throat, the boy who oozes now, but didn't ooze then. Your other "friends" stopped trying to kill you, trying to bury you alive in the sandbox adjacent to the playground when the tumors used your eyes to look at them like you could open their throats. Though they saved you that day, you keep quelling your tumors's bloodlust with pill after pill after pill.

❧

You can't remember when you have never been at war with your own body, when your legs were not plagued with psoriasis, when you walked instead of hopped. Unlike the boy who coughs up oil, you figured out how to make yourself a myth, a myth boys died for while sailing the seas, how they would fall off their ships and wait for your adopted kind to save them from drowning and would realize too late when your kind never came, their lungs filling with saltwater and panic, a myth boys that would make landlocked boys chase after you, even though you did not know or want them to chase after you, you just wanted to be something more than a girl with fused legs and psoriasis.

The first time you told your best friend, the girl with the melting face, the truth about your fused legs and psoriasis, it was during a sleepover in third grade, shortly after you came out to your class that you were really a mermaid, and your best friend backed your claim. When you told her the truth, she said it was ok for her to lie how she wasn't a mermaid, she was just a girl with fused legs and psoriasis. The girl with the melting face said you were an ocean boys might drown in, if they weren't careful. *You don't have to save them,* she said. *All I want you to do is swim around them.*

23

You remember the first war you were ever in. Your ninth grade class declared war on the tenth grade class. The principal didn't even ask your class to do it. Your class vice-president, the boy who oozes, decided that the tenth graders were mooching off the school resources and needed to be made examples of, to use their bodies as resources, and your president, the girl with half a face, agreed. Your tumors started waking from their chemically induced slumber, stoked the bloodlust in your fists, in your heart, but you volunteered to work in the nurse's office, helped treat wounds on both sides. The boy who oozes wanted you executed for your treason, your betrayal against your fellow classmates but the president refused. *We need boys and girls like him to patch people up*, she said. *You can't fight a war without willing bodies.* The boy who oozes appealed her ruling to the Student Body Supreme Court and upheld the president's ruling; it was the first time the law was on your side. It might be the only time the law saved your life.

The school forbade students having guns, and it didn't make sense in this country where the American god is in every gun in every hand that holds one until the principal reminded the warring factions that guns are for adults, and they will get to use one when they turn 18 and have graduated. You learned to not cringe as much as the casualties were wheeled inside the nurse's office: heads caved with baseball bats, torsos turned into sieves, a smiling stomach or two. *This could happen to us*, you reminded your tumors and all they could say back is *so?*

❧

You first noticed the boy who coughs up oil during the war between your ninth grade class and the tenth grade class. All the girls in your grade had to take turns helping the wounded piling up in the nurse's office and the boy who coughs up oil was the only boy you saw helping the wounded. You asked him why he wasn't out there fighting with the rest of the boys, why he wasn't helping the ninth graders secure their future until they graduate, and he said he was helping them by patching up the wounded enough so they could go back out there and fight, or at least act as human shields. You notice he also helped with the tenth grade wounded and you asked him why and he said they deserve a chance, too. *They didn't ask for this war, remember?* You stood there stunned at his conviction, his willingness to do what was right rather than what was easy.

The ninth grade soldiers promised you teeth, eyes, and ears of their enemies, promised to make you trophies out of the blood they've spilled, the bodies they've left behind to mark you as their next conquest and you did your best to blush honestly, as if to make them believe that the best way to your heart is through murder, through victory, through patriotism, so they would not make you their next conquest. You began incubating a crush on the boy who coughs up oil late at night when you and your mother's wine could be alone.

24

Your tumors encourage you to keep going with your piecemeal wingman project, and you know more than you ever knew that you can't trust them to do right by you anymore, that they are out for themselves. You've been able to keep them quiet, muzzle their voices, their desire to hijack your body so they can carry out their plans, indulge in their whims, like wooing the girl whose mouth opens sideways or beating other boys into useless meat. Tripling your dosage has calmed the tumors down, but you feel their pull more and more on your mouth, on your limbs. You feel the rising tide of bloodlust, and the pills are just a finger in the cracks of your resolve. You feel the bloodlust leak drip by drip on your bones and muscle.

You ask your father if you can go to the doctor and see if he can do anything about the growing autonomy of your tumors, and your father asks if you're sure you want to do that, and you nod. Your father pulls the .38 Special that's been passed down from father to son for four generations and he asks where you want the bullet this time, since the state only treats your illness when a bullet is involved. You say clavicle, and before your father can aim and fire, you watch your arms lunge for the gun. In one clean motion, your hands disarm your father. You watch yourself aim the .38 Special that's been passed down from father to son for four generations. *What are you doing*, you ask your tumors, and they reply, *the right thing*.

❥

You don't care what the rest of the class thinks when you rush to the hospital after hearing on the news how the boy who coughs up oil's father was shot in his own home. You were afraid that the boy who oozes escalated the war too much, too soon, by ordering a hit on the boy who coughs up oil's father to punish the boy who coughs up oil for his refusal to become a brick in a wall to heaven that keeps boys like him out of it, keeps girls like you safe from boys like him in the afterlife. You stop when you see the boy who coughs up oil in the ER waiting room, his face buried in his hands, crying. You ask him why he isn't with his father right now and he looks up at you, eyes wet with regret, and he says that his father's in surgery, and the nurse told him to wait here until the doctors were done in surgery. You ask the boy who coughs up oil what happened and he starts to move his mouth to tell you before his body locks up. You watch his face twitch and twitch. He slaps himself once and then twice, and his face won't stop twitching. The arm attached to the hand slapping his cheek drops to his side, dead. He looks down at the linoleum floor, takes a couple of breaths, and then looks up at you. *We did what we had to do*, he said, and you notice how he uses "we" instead of "I".

25

You think about the time your father taught how to ride a bike, how he didn't give up on you even as you fell over and over again, plaguing your body with scrapes and bruises, saying the same swears your father says when he's trying to fix or fight something and was losing to the thing he tried to fix or fight. After you rode around the block a few times without falling, without new bruising or bleeding, you asked your father why his father was added to the border wall, why a good man like your grandfather could pass down patience to your father, why would he be punished. *It's not a punishment,* your father said, *it's an honor to be part of the wall that protects us from the hordes that threaten our way of life. It was the only way your grandfather could serve this country and it'll be the only way I can serve this country, other than raising a son.* You coughed up something oily and wiped it on your overalls. You asked whether you would live long enough to be part of the wall and your father answered *hopefully, if you're in a winnable war.* You think about the bullet bouncing around your father's stomach and you pray and pray and pray that the American god will protect your father, save. You'd rather have a father be a brick in the border wall than as a seed planted beneath the ground, a body waiting for someone to loot it.

You point out to the boy who coughs up oil how he referred himself as "we" and "I", and he tries taking it back in a voice that isn't his and you give him the look you've given other boys when they're lying, the look that is known throughout the school to break a lie in half and even in this state, the boy who coughs up oil admits you caught them in a lie, that she, their host's beloved mermaid, is speaking to them, not him. You ask them, *where is the boy who coughs up oil,* and they tell you, *thinking about his father, praying to his American god that his father will*

 You ask, *why would the boy who coughs up oil shoot his father*, and they said, *he didn't shoot him, we did. We shot his father to cover our tracks. Our takeover of our host's body is almost complete, but one thing is stopping us: you. His love for you is the only thing holding us back from erasing him and becoming what we have always wanted to be: an American ready to make the weak bleed at a moment's notice, an American maintaining the road tó freedom with every bullet, with every body they leave behind, a good American.* You look them in their eyes and slap the boy who coughs up oil once on each cheek. *You'll have to do better*, they say. You take his face in your hands and you kiss the boy who coughs up oil slow and deep. When you're finished, the boy who coughs up oil looks at you and asks *what happened?*

26

You wait until your mother is asleep before going down to the basement and locking the door so she can't walk in on you as you have a conversation with your tumors. You gather the largest gob of phlegm you can in your throat and spit in the half there face of your piecemeal wingman. You smear the oily phlegm all over the half there face of your piecemeal wingman making sure the phlegm gets into the skin, the half there jaw bone. You ask the half there face of your piecemeal wingman, *what did they do*, and it says *we finally got you the kiss you've been boiling for since you first saw the mermaid treating wounded ninth and tenth graders in the nurse's office. We got tired of your indecision, your convoluted plans to build this piecemeal wingman you've got us talking to you from to distract the mermaid's best friend, the girl with the melting face.* You slap the half there face of your piecemeal wingman and yell how this was not the way you wanted your first kiss to come from the mermaid, not to break some sort of spell that they, the tumors, put him under after they shot his father. *You need to embrace the monster you really are,* the half there face of your piecemeal wingman says. *The sooner you do, the happier you'll be.* You try to slap the half there face of your piecemeal wingman but the tumors stop your arm before you have a chance to lift it.

❥

You don't know what got into you when the tumors said to you through the mouth of the boy who coughs up oil's love for you that was holding them back from taking over his body. You being a mermaid are required to break curses, even though mermaids are more cursed than men to live beneath the ocean and wait for them to sail by to tease them with the promise of your mouth on theirs, the promise of their mouth on your neck, the promise of their hands running up and down your tail, feeling your scales, how your kind would drown them then sort through the bodies to figure out which ones had the right legs to transplant tail and fin. There was no one in the ER to challenge your validity as a mermaid, whether the myth of you could break the spell the boy who coughs up oil was under. You didn't need to kiss him but something in your heart or the full moon of your hormones said you had to, you had to stake your claim on his body when the tumors challenged your dominance, when they said that they almost owned him, almost. What you didn't expect was the coppery aftertaste in the boy's mouth, like when you tried once to see if you could suck the energy out of a battery and use the current to burn away the scaly psoriasis running up and down your fused legs. You tried rinsing it out with water, then toothpaste, then mouthwash, then a sip of your mother's stolen wine, and your mouth finally begins to feel normal again.

27

You think about how you can earn a kiss from your beloved mermaid honestly, without your tumors challenging her for dominance, without a wounded father to encourage the mermaid to wet nurse your feelings, your guilt. The piecemeal wingman project is no longer feasible. All of those late nights you spent digging up parts and pieces of boys to stitch into the perfect wingman to distract the mermaid's best friend, the girl with the melting face, so you and the mermaid could be alone more often, have allowed your tumors to multiply and metastasize, and take over your body. You should have known better to trust them to pilot your body when you could no longer stay awake. You're aware of what your body has done in the past when you slept, and the tumors played puppeteer, but you're afraid of those moments that you could become unaware of, where you wake up in strange places and ask your tumors where you are and what have they done, and they won't need to answer you because they've made your body theirs and your body your prison where all you can do is watch how they use your body to accomplish their objectives. You used to think your tumors wanted to kill you, as most tumors do, and you're not sure what they really want, other than to love the girl whose mouth opens sideways, maybe use you to metastasize in her, start a pandemic one boy, one girl at a time.

You're not sure if you want to be more than just friends with the boy who coughs oil. You feel the tumors are suckering you into the boy who coughs up oil's arms, dangling a broken boy in front of you like bait, as if the tumors sense your need to nurture, as if the tumors sense your inherent desire to conquer the right boy, stake your claim with your hands, your mouth, your body. You don't like what you become when you're under the full moon of your hormones, this thirsty creature. You wonder whether the boy who coughs up oil wants help in defeating his tumors, you as the prize, you as the princess in the other other other other other other other (other) castle waiting for him to slay the monster of his body and bring himself to you like a trophy. Your best friend, the girl with the melting face, thinks the idea of you and the boy who coughs oil forming a *we* entity is a terrible idea, and you only half believe her. The other half knows the girl with the melting face loves you as more than a friend and would say anything to poison your flickering desire for anyone and everyone but her. You pour some of your mother's stolen wine into a glass and sip and ask your less sober reflection in the mirror what you should do about your flickering desire for the boy who coughs oil, and you feel the water rising between your ears.

28

You forgot today you would be 16 going on 17 when you came downstairs to the kitchen and you found a cupcake with a candle stabbed in it, the wick unlit, a wrapped present and a note: light it yourself. You know the lettering is your mother's because it's in cursive. You can tell she's still angry about you shooting your father, her husband, in the stomach, how he's still in the hospital recovering from not just the bullet, but the tumors they found in his body. You now know where you got the architecture to grow up as a greenhouse of cancer, except his tumors probably don't talk to him like yours talk to you. They are ordinary tumors designed by the American god to weed out the weak, so the teacher tells you during your Science lessons, how your god, the American god, has American interests in mind when he (always he, only he) made America and the people living on it. You open up the present first and see it's a new bootleg cassette. Your father's block lettering tells you this cassette contains pornography and you had to read it twice to confirm that it says pornography on it. You don't even bother lighting the candle. You run upstairs, put the cassette in your stereo, and put your headphones on. You don't want your mother to hear the moaning you might be hearing, the grunting, the sweating that you'd like to do with the mermaid (if or when she's ready and she finds you worthy of grunting and sweating over) and you realize it's not that kind of pornography when you hear how it doesn't matter if we all die.

❧

You realize today is the boy who coughs oil's birthday and you decide to stay home and delay dealing with conundrum your heart, your brain, and your hormones have put you in when it comes to your feelings for the boy who coughs oil. Your best friend, the girl with the melting face, probably went to school and won't be around, as she is trying to be the first girl in 20 years to be school valedictorian. You forgot to hide the empty wine bottle on your desk when your mother walks into your bedroom to find out why you aren't out of bed, why you aren't heading out to school. You fake moan as if you're sick, and you watch your mother walk over to the empty wine bottle and look into it to confirm it is empty, and she says you really need to drink a glass of water between each glass of wine. You watch her pick up the empty wine bottle and walk out of your bedroom with it. You peel the covers off of your fused legs and swing yourself upright. You stare at your closed bedroom door and wished your mother would act like a real mother and chide you for not only stealing her wine, but drinking it as well. It's as if she wants you to be like her and drink yourself to death glass by glass to punish you for your existence, your transformation from girl to mermaid chasing your father away.

29

Today, the teacher on the American History VHS tape reminds the class how America became great again when America embraced the American god and vowed to come together and be the hands and feet of this perfect (white) American god to choke and stomp out all other gods who do not believe that the American god is the right god. The teacher reminds you, and the class, how the smog we breathe is the exhale of this American god and because we Americans breathe him in every day, we are a vital part of this American god, even when we are dead, we are a vital part of this American god, and now it is time for everyone to bow their heads and give thanks to this American god. The guard gestures with his AK-47 and you and the class bow their heads but you aren't praying to the American god because you don't believe in him, what his breath and his actions have done to your body, to the other mutated boys and girls you know, but you can hear your tumors praising the American god, giving thanks to him for their existence, giving thanks to him for the host body that they are about to take over, giving thanks to him for giving them the strength to be the pandemic they've been dreaming about since their host body was in his mother's womb. You hear their prayers and know that you may need to not sleep as much until your father gets out of the hospital and you can steal his pills to keep your tumors quiet.

You put your head down when the teacher on the American History VHS tape commanded that everyone in the class give thanks to the American god, the only god worthy to watch over this world and the heaven beyond this world known as America but you stopped believing in this god, the American god, after your father left you and your mother, your legs freshly fused, the psoriasis on your legs freshly bloomed. Your father didn't have the courage to let the bullet burrow through your body so the doctor could find it and then take a look at your legs, your psoriasis, and figure out why your body was doing this, turning you into a landlocked mermaid. You remember bits and pieces how your father tried handing your mother the gun and your mother shoved the gun back in your father's hands, yelling how it was his job to provide for the family, how our god, the American god, empowers him to give life and take it because it's a man's job to be the alpha and the omega, per our god, the American god. You remember bits and pieces how you felt your father's lips on your forehead before he walked out of the house one last time. You know the consequences of not acknowledging or worshiping or praising the American god so you thank him for the mythology of your body, of being the type of girl boys think about when they go off to the best war and kill for their country, kill for the American god.

30

You dream of being in a classroom by yourself and rather than a teacher teaching from the comfort and safety of a VHS tape, it's an actual live teacher writing his name on an actual blackboard with actual chalk. You haven't seen a live teacher or a blackboard or chalk since you were in sixth grade, the last grade they allowed actual teachers to teach students before boys and girls begin to succumb to the full moon of their hormones. The teacher doesn't say anything though. He (maybe he based on the shape of his body from the back) keeps trying to write his name and then erases it. After he does this seven times, you yell "hey." You yell *mister, hey mister*. You ask if he's ok and he keeps trying to write his name and then erases it, as if he's more focused on that than on you. You finally get out of your desk, walk over to the teacher. You tap him on his shoulder and he keeps trying to write his name and erases it. You put your hand on his shoulder and he keeps trying to write his name and then erases it. You grab his left forearm, the arm he writes and erases with, and he struggles to keep writing and erasing, and then finally gives up. He drops the chalk and turns to look at you. You reel back as you stare into the face of the half face of your piecemeal wingman. *How may I help you*, he asks, and you wake us with a baseball bat in your hand, the bat hovering over your sleeping mother.

❧

You have that dream again where you are swimming in the ocean, your two arms and two legs working together to help you swim around and around and around. You hear your father yell for you to come to shore and you make your way to the beach, the muscles in your arms and legs burning. You stretch, open your arms wide so your body can collect energy from a sun that isn't killing you like the sun does now on days where perpetual summer becomes a low feverish hell. You walk over to your mother and father reclining in their beach chairs. Your father throws you a towel and you dry yourself off. When you take a good look at your father, you see his perfect body but his face isn't there. His head is there turning and talking as if it had a face, but you can't hear what he's saying to your mother. You feel a hand on your shoulder and you turn and see the boy who oozes, the bodies of dead boys behind him. *I did this for you,* he says, *I did this to show your parents how much I love you. Your father was so impressed, he helped make these boys into bricks,* and you look at the fresh blood on your father's hands, the blood on your mother in the shape of your father's hands. You wake up, your mouth packed with wool. You pick up the wine bottle you drained of all its wine and look through it for a future better than this.

31

The American Science teacher on the VHS tape introduces a documentary on how the American god forced us to finally take up arms against America's greatest enemy: anything that would dare impede American progress. You watch birds copied from a computer and pasted into the real world attack everyone indiscriminately, and the only thing that could save Americans from this nightmare is the holy spirit of the American god: the bullet. You watch how bullet after bullet fells the birds and the birds don't so much fall to the earth and become things to be picked clean but explode as if they filled their bellies with explosives so even after they die, whatever is around them will join them in their heaven, bird heaven. The American Science teacher comes back on after the documentary finishes and asks everyone what they learned and provides the address to mail those answers and the date that the answers must be mailed by to prevent the in-classroom guard from deducting a knee cap, a lung, or any other organ or bone his bullet deems worthy of punishment. You think your answer will be that the father aspect of the American god thought it would be a good idea to blanket America in his exhale after he watched the bravery of those men and women who took up arms against that which would impede American progress, how his exhale would be a preemptive action so those brave Americans could take up arms against other things that would impede American progress. Man versus man is the best American conflict, you've been taught to believe.

You try to hide your disgust over the alleged documentary you're watching in American Science class, the one where nature rebels against American progress and American values by sending in flocks of suicide bombers to kill Americans for their contributions to the environment and you can't. You resist putting your head down because it will encourage the guard to summon the holy spirit of the American god to enter you in a bone or an organ of the American god's choosing. You correct your face and enter a place in your mind where you think of more important things, like what you and your best friend, the girl with the melting face, will be doing on Friday night instead of going to the Homecoming dance, the first school sanctioned dating event of the school year. Many boys asked for your hand, your waist, and you refused them all. The one boy who you might say *yes* to, the boy who coughs oil, didn't even bother to try and you couldn't blame him: he shot his father and fights for control of his own body. You and your best friend will probably steal a bottle or two of your mother's wine and go swimming with each sip. You'll dive deep in the ocean of your feelings and discover the wreckage beneath and drag it out to the shore for the two of you to inspect, figure out whether what to melt the wreckage into or whether to walk away from it all.

32

The banners hanging in every hallway remind you that Friday is the Homecoming dance, the first school sanctioned dating event of the school year. There used to be a football game the night before but the school district decided that boys needed to be healthy for actual wars with actual American interests at stake instead of simulated wars with school pride at stake. You kick yourself for forgetting about Homecoming. You try blaming your tumors for removing the day from your memory and they say it isn't their fault that you forgot and for the first time in a long time, you believe them. You think better of asking the mermaid out to Homecoming. The ground between you two is unsteady. The mermaid only kissed you to break the hold your tumors had over your body in the hospital. The bullet the doctor dug out of your father reminds you how you don't deserve anything good. Your tumors lust for the girl whose mouth opens sideways and would propel your body towards her, move your mouth, and use your words to ask her out to Homecoming. At night, you slip more and more into the dreams of your tumors, the pandemic they want to become, a singularity spread throughout the world one body at a time. You can feel your tumors assault the dam of monogamy you've built around your heart.

The boy who oozes slithers up to you while you and your best friend, the girl with the melting face, talk to each other next to her locker. The boy who oozes is surrounded by his security detail of hall monitors. He says you will go with him to Homecoming through the border wall of his security detail. You ask two of the boys in front of the boy who oozes if they could step aside for a moment so he can get a better look at the gratitude in your eyes, and the boy who oozes nods and they step aside. You poke his chest with your finger and you tell him that no boy orders her to go anywhere with him, that your permission must be earned. The boy who oozes reminds you that he can turn the boy who coughs oil into a brick in the wall he wants to build around heaven, and you ask how that worked out the last time the boy who oozes tried that. The boy who oozes stands there, mouth agape, skin oozing more than normal. One of the hall monitors finally closes the boy who oozes's mouth by pushing up his jaw. He looks at the hall monitor who closed his mouth and nods, and that hall monitor takes his baton out of his holster and pins your best friend against the lockers, the baton digging in her throat, her face melting faster. *Say yes,* the boy who oozes yells. *Say yes.*

33

You see the mermaid's best friend, the girl with the melting face, wearing a neck brace. You stop her in the hallway and ask what happened. She asks whether your concern is genuine or whether you're trying to score points with the mermaid, and you say your concern is genuine. The girl with the melting face says she doesn't entirely believe you but will tell you anyway. She asks you whether you knew the mermaid was going to Homecoming with the boy who oozes and you shake your head. You say how you've got a lot going on at home and the girl with the melting face nods as if she knows, which she probably does since the mermaid is her best friend. The girl with the melting face says that the mermaid did it to save her life. The girl with the melting face takes a step back when she sees your eyes blacken, and you're not sure if your tumors are doing it or if you are. *Did he touch you,* you mouth asks but the voice doesn't sound like yours, and the girl with the melting face says *no, one of the hall monitors did it. I couldn't see his face since the hall monitors wear blacked out visors.* You or your tumors imagine the boy who oozes's blood in your mouth, what's left of his throat between your teeth. *She's not worth a war,* the girl with the melting face yells as you storm down the hallway.

The boy who coughs up oil is a blur of black clothes and gangly limbs as he runs down the hallway. He doesn't stop when he's close to one of the hall monitors detailed to protect the class president. You watch the boy who coughs up oil spear the hall monitor with his shoulder, drilling him into the floor. Everyone, including you, stops to watch the boy who coughs up oil rip off the blacked out visor protecting the hall monitor's face and identity. *What do you want,* the hall monitor says, scared. Everyone, including you, hears the boy who coughs up oil gather the phlegm in his throat. He spits something oily in the hall monitor's face and it causes everyone, including you, to cringe. You can see the boy who coughs up oil rub the oily phlegm in the hall monitor's face. The hall monitor tries to put up his hands but every time he does, the boy who coughs up oil slaps the hall monitor's face, and keeps rubbing the oily phlegm in the hall monitor's eyes, nose, and mouth. You gather the courage to walk over and put your hand on the boy who coughs up oil's shoulders. *What do you want*, the tumors ask through his mouth. You ask the tumors to stop doing what they are doing, and they ask you why should they when someone like him hurt her best friend, and you're stunned for a moment the tumors care about her and you and not the girl whose mouth opens sideways. *Promise us you won't tell him what happened*, the tumors say, and you're not sure if you can.

34

You wake up in the nurse's office, your left shoulder aching. You look at your hands and feel your knuckles throb. You look at your palms and notice the stain of your oily phlegm on them. You ask your tumors what they did and they don't know what you're talking about. You try to access the lost minutes but your tumors stop you in the shape of a stern librarian. *Why won't you let me see*, you ask and the librarian shushes you, orders you to sleep and you fight the weight of your eyelids. You fight the sand filling your limbs. You order your body to stand and the librarian hushes your muscles. *What are you not telling me*, you ask your tumors again, and you feel them gathering in your chest to pin you to the slab they call a bed. You give in and shut your eyes and you begin to hear a voice that isn't yours but no one is in the nurse's office, not even the nurse. You try to ask who's there but some of your tumors gather around your mouth to muzzle you. You focus on the voice that isn't yours and you begin to recognize it. You get bits and pieces of you having a hall monitor pinned on the ground, you sitting on his chest, the hall monitor pleading for his life. Before you can see what happened next, the librarian hushes you, orders you to dream, and you finally do.

❧

You tell your best friend what happened with the boy who coughs up oil and the hall monitor, and her face stops melting for a moment to express her shock that the boy who coughs up oil would do something like that. *He must really like you if he's willing to start a war*, she says, and you say that it was his body but not him, and your best friend looks at you, confused. She asks: *how could it be his body and not him?* Before you can answer, you feel a hand on your shoulder, and it spins you around, and you look into the blacked out visor of one of the faceless hall monitors. He demands you come with him and drags you away by your shirt to a vacant hallway. The hall monitor throws you into an empty handicapped bathroom and locks the door. He orders you to sit on the toilet and you refuse. The hall monitor removes his helmet and blacked out visor, and you see the hall monitor weep something oily constantly, the same kind of oil your (maybe) future boyfriend coughs up. He reminds you how you promised them, the boy who coughs up oil's tumors, to not say anything about what they did and she was about to break that promise. You ask what would happen if you told your best friend the truth, and the hall monitor points to his eyes and says she would be next.

35

Your tumors take on the form of your father when you confront them in this in-between state they have put you in, as if the sight and sounds of your father will stop you from fighting them. *We know what's best for you,* your tumors in the skin of your father say. *You will be the new American god when we have spread all over this country. We promise to keep the mermaid free of us so you can win her the right way, through your own words and your own deeds. All you have to do is trust us.* Before you can respond, you feel something wet on your lips, something wet and pressing for fifteen seconds, then thirty seconds, then a minute, and you open your eyes on your own and see your mouth connected to the mermaid's. She stops kissing you when your eyes meet, and she takes a hop or two back. *Who am I talking to,* the mermaid asks, and you say, *me,* and she hugs you, whispering in your ear how it worked.

❧

You were surprised the tumors inhabiting the hall monitor let you out of the handicapped bathroom intact. They could have possessed you right then and there, your memories, your eyes becoming oily dark, but your absence or their control over you could be the thing that drives their host to kill himself. Without their host being alive, the boy who coughs up oil becomes their coffin. The tumors though are smart enough to know that putting your best friend in danger is the best way to keep you in check. You know you will tell your best friend what's going on, eventually. You have to figure out how to do it without getting caught. First things first though, you run to the nurse's office where the boy who coughs up oil should be after his fight with the hall monitor. You see through the glass and wire pane of the nurse's office that the boy who coughs oil lays on an examination slab. You knock on the glass to see if the nurse comes or your hand knocking on the glass will wake up the boy who coughs up oil, and the nurse doesn't come, and the boy who coughs up oil doesn't stir. You try the door handle and it twists and allows you to open the door. You close the door behind you. You walk over to the boy who coughs up oil, take his face in your hands, and you kiss him. When he wakes up, you hug him and whisper *it worked*.

36

You look at the spell breaking eyes, and the spell breaking face, and the spell breaking mouth of the mermaid after she breaks the hold (again) of your tumors. You sit up on the examination slab, your legs dangling from the side. You wonder if this is the right time to ask the mermaid whether she would go to Homecoming with you. One of your tumors, the one that relocated beneath your left ear, cheers you on as you hurtle towards the mermaid's open arms and (maybe) the mermaid's open mouth. You ask that tumor why it's cheering you on, slipping the question beneath your tongue, and that tumor says it just wants you to be happy, unlike the other tumors who only want to break you so they can be the pandemic the American god made them to be. You don't trust the double agency of your body, what the full moon of hormones turns you into. You remember how your father fed you a diet of what not to do with girls when he showed you that bootlegged sitcom about the family with a comically intolerable nerd living next door who had a crush on the family's oldest daughter and would not stop wooing her even after she said no for the seventieth time, the nerd proclaiming how he was wearing his beloved down. Your father said don't be like the nerd and you nodded and agreed. You look at the mermaid and thank her for saving you again.

As you hug the boy who coughs up oil, the dating part of your brain hopes he wouldn't do that stupid thing boys do after you rescue them and mistake your care for their well being to be something that means like or love, where your bodies count the minutes and hours and days until you can feel and taste each other again. So many wounded boys during the great ninth grade war wanted you as more than their nurse, you patched them up and put them back to fight for the future of their class. They would come back to you and present trophies of teeth or other things they managed to pry from their enemies after vanquishing them, as if the right trophy would unlock your heart, your arms, and your mouth, and when you refused them, they wouldn't take no for an answer and the trophies grew into a shrine in front of your locker. The lie of your mermaid biology already made you more myth than girl, but your refusal of their trophies made the moon of their hormones glow, drove your would be suitors into a frenzy, and they kept killing and killing and you kept saying no. You got them to finally stop when you said that to love you, they had to find a boy who would love your best friend, and you knew the impossibility of that task because she loves you as more than a friend. The boy who coughs up oil at least knows better and only thanks you for saving him, again.

37

You swallow all of the pills you have left to see whether it cripples your tumors or kills you (finally). Your esophagus closes in mid swallow, and you gasp for air, making huck huck huck sounds. You are alone in the house with your mother at work and your father being treated for the kind of tumors you wish you had, ones that would kill you instead of use you. You fight everything in you to not let your tumors save your life (again), but your tumors win that argument and pilot you into the bathroom. You feel the water stopper in the sink in your fingers as your tumors command your hand to twist it off. You feel the grime caked on the plastic part of the water stopper as your hand pulls it out of the drain. Your tumors ram you again and again against the edge of the bathroom sink until the pills explode out of your mouth and down the open drain. Your tumors make your hands turn the cold faucet all the way to make sure the pills go down the drain. You cough up something oily onto the bathroom mirror and you draw a face on the mirror with your phlegm. *There are too many of us now*, the face on the mirror says. *You cannot stop the new American god we are becoming* and you mar the face on the mirror to the stain it should be.

You and a bottle of your mother's wine sneak into your best friend's bedroom. Your best friend brings the bottle inside before she pulls you through the open window. *What's the occasion*, your best friend asks, and you say you're here to toast her survival and to apologize for saying yes to going to Homecoming with the boy who oozes. Your best friend grabs two paper cups from her bathroom and you fill them with your mother's wine. *What happened to the hall monitor your boyfriend beat up*, your best friend asks, and you give her a look that reminds her how the boy who coughs up oil isn't your boyfriend. *I still wanna know what*

happened, she asks, and you say she might not believe her if you told her the truth. *Is this about your boyfriend's tumors?* You nod. *How bad is it?* You find a sheet of paper and write: they're spreading across the school. You ball up the paper, shove it in your mouth, chew the ball of paper until you can swallow it. You chase the chewed paper with wine. Your best friend looks at you in shock either because you told her the boy who coughs up oil's tumors are spreading through the school or because you ate paper in front of her for the first time since second grade.

38

You heard on one of the bootleg music tapes your dad gave you how love is suicide and you wish your like (maybe love if you are lucky and the mermaid agrees that she could fall in love with you one day, too) could kill you to end this perpetual war you've been in with your body since the doctor found the tumor growing on your lung after he removed the bullet from your leg, the one your father put in you after you told him you coughed up something oily, and the bullet being the only way the doctor sees you, all other diagnoses second to the bullet burrowed in a body part or a bone broken because of the bullet. You were taught to believe in the religion portion of your elementary school education that being hit with a bullet is like being touched by the American god, how the more it hurts, the more he purifies you, cleansing you of all things un-American. Suicide is un-American, the posters throughout school remind you, the ones that were put up after 12 boys and 6 girls in your class killed themselves last summer; you were born to die for the American god and no one else, not even yourself. *We know what you're thinking*, one of your tumors says. *We will stop you if you try again.*

You and your best friend try to figure how to stop the boy who coughs up oil's tumors from spreading further inside the school. Your best friend suggests the most obvious solution, killing the boy who coughs up oil the same way the herd is thinned in the city that used to be called Atlanta, open his head and let his life spill out for the birds to peck and the bugs to gnaw on but you don't have the stomach to have the boy who coughs up oil's blood on your hands. You've had blood of a dying boy on your hands once and that was once too many. Your best friend suggests that neither she nor you be the one who kills the boy who coughs up oil but one of the hall monitors protecting the class president, and you're not sure that's a good idea. While you are underwater with wine, you cannot remember which hall monitor the tumors hijacked. They all wear the same outfits, cover their faces the same, their heights and builds similar enough to be all the same boy unless more than one of them are in the same room. The full moon of your hormones pulls you in the direction of the boy who coughs up oil as the tumors turn him into a local American god, a god your body wants but your brain knows the danger the school is in, so you quell the tyranny of your desire and tell your best friend you'll warn the class president of what's coming and see what he does.

39

When you (or your tumors make you) drift off to sleep during class, you see another classroom, with the American Algebra teacher on TV talking about how to calculate a body count during a war where American lives are lost, how the bodies with the non-preferred skin color aren't factored in. The Math teacher says this is how we can show the American god how much we are winning by how much we aren't losing. You watch hands that aren't yours write on paper that isn't yours take note of this American arithmetic. You watch a hand that isn't yours raise and hear a voice that isn't yours ask how do we know what skin color the American god doesn't prefer and the guard with his gleaming, oiled AK-47 answers the bodies where bullets make nests and give birth to more bullets. The voice that isn't yours asks, *so if the bullet passes through the body, then the American god favors that skin color*, and the guard shrugs and says, *ask your Algebra teacher when you mail your homework and he'll tell you.* You watch hands that aren't yours make note of the guard's response. You listen to thoughts that aren't yours wander off into his schedule protecting the class president, how he wishes the president wasn't so aggressive about building a wall around heaven. You watch through eyes that aren't yours how the classroom and the TV change into monochromatic hues.

❧

You inspect the ash ringing around your eyes, kiss tissue after tissue to make sure your mouth is a lure to shed clothing in dark, damp places. You can't remember the last time you wore a face that would cause men to jump in the ocean to kiss you, how you would race them to the bottom, and promise them your lips if they kept up though none of them ever could. You're not looking to negotiate with the boy who oozes about the safety of the school and the wellbeing of his constituents, the eleventh grade class. You want him to obey your command, crook your finger like a leash to bring the class president to heel, to save all of the school from the menace growing from the boy who coughs up oil's body. You look at yourself in the mirror and say to yourself over and over again that you are doing the right thing by putting the safety and wellbeing of the school before your happiness. You don't have the stomach to kill the boy who coughs up oil. The full moon of your hormones makes you want to do the opposite, find dark and damp places for you and the boy who coughs up oil to touch each other. You look at yourself in the mirror, the mermaid you have become for this moment, count the hearts you'll have to break before this battle is through. You drown the tyranny of your desire with a sip of your mother's wine before you head off to class.

40

You come to standing in front of your bathroom mirror and notice you're wearing your best white dress shirt and jeans, a yet-to-be knotted plain black necktie around your popped collar. You gather as much phlegm as you can and spit it on the bathroom mirror. You give the oily glob two eyes and a mouth. *What am I doing here*, you ask, and the face says: *getting ready for Homecoming*. You don't remember asking anyone to go with you, especially the mermaid who has saved you from yourself now twice. You ask the face how long you haven't had control of your body and it says: *long enough*. You try accessing what your tumors did through the puppetry of your body and they won't let you. You ask the face what the tumors are hiding from you and it says: *trust us, we know what's best for us, what's best for you*. You feel your tumors gather around your shoulders to simulate reassuring hands on them. The face says: *tonight begins their first step in becoming the new American god and all who come to Homecoming will bear witness to our ascension*. You ask the face what about the mermaid and it says: *no harm will come to her unless she interferes with our plans*. You watch your hands tie the necktie and fix your collar. The face says: *we can let you watch*, if you want, and you nod.

❧

The boy who oozes laughs when you tell him how the boy who coughs up oil's tumors are planning to take over the school one boy, one girl at a time. He laughs again when you use the word "pandemic" to describe what could happen if the boy who coughs up oil's tumors have their way. You say that you'll be the boy who oozes's date to Homecoming, and he reminds you how you already surrendered to the charms of his hall monitor's baton when you saved your best friend from being choked to death. You say that you'll make an effort to enjoy his company, to make it look like to everyone else in the cafetorium turned ballroom that you belong to him. He leans back, stunned, when you say that you'll make an effort to enjoy his company, as if it finally dawned on him that maybe, just maybe, you aren't interested in him. The boy who oozes runs his runny fingers through his runny hair, and says he wants more than just your simulated joy, but the trophy of your body, to find a dark and damp place and howl at the full moon of each other's hormones, to know the ache of him for hours and days after it's over. He says only then if you agree to give him everything that he'll protect the school from the boy who coughs up oil. You slap the boy who oozes, first on the right cheek, then on the left; you'd rather see the school under the reign of the boy who coughs up oil's tumors than have your body haunted by the boy who oozes for the rest of your life.

41

Your tumors allow you to marvel at the cafetorium's wondrous transformation into an undersea palace, this year's theme for Homecoming, the first school sanctioned dating event of the school year. You have a feeling that the boy who oozes pulled strings and had enough bones broken to make sure Homecoming would be perfect for the mermaid. You seethe beneath the full moon of your hormones when you think of the boy who oozes touching the mermaid. *This anger is good,* your tumors say. *Why won't you work with us in our transformation to destroy your romantic rival?* You tell your tumors how violence doesn't solve anything and they remind you that if it wasn't for violence, your father wouldn't have met your mother. You tell them that proves your point, how your existence doesn't solve anything, and the tumors disagree. They remind you to not do anything stupid if you don't want them harm the mermaid, and you nod to show them that you agree not to do anything stupid but you know you want to do something stupid, anything to stop the tumors from doing what they need to do to begin their transformation into the new American god.

❧

You pour some of your mother's wine for yourself and the girl with the melting face. You and her giggle at the makeover warpaint each of you wear on your faces. Part of you feels guilty for not going to Homecoming, but you couldn't stomach hanging from the boy who oozes's arm, even to try to save everyone else from the boy who oozes's tumors. After her second mug of wine, the girl with the melting face asks why didn't you go, knowing what you know, and you say you can't be the one who always saves the boy who coughs up oil from himself. Your best friend stares at you as if she doesn't know who you are. You pour her more wine and then take another sip from your mug.

You know if something happened while you were there, something you couldn't stop, no one else would be able to tell those who did not go the truth of what happened. You tell your best friend you feel for everyone who went to Homecoming, what might be coming for them, but better them than you and her, how guilt is a luxury survivors can afford. This underwater version of yourself is callous, but practical.

42

You wake up in the back of an ambulance, your insides burning. It's a burning you're all too familiar with after someone plants bullets inside of you, or the bullets burrow through your body and plant themselves in something or someone else. You used your anger the way your tumors suggested, but not the way they wanted. You used their strength and fury to take out several of the hall monitors guarding the boy who oozes. In their excitement, the tumors forgot that the school forbade student-on-student violence during school sanctioned dating events. The school knew bruises and blood would turn off girls, would stop them from thinking things like the possibility of going steady, of marriage down the line, of birthing children to continue making America worthy in the eyes of the American god. The rules state you receive one warning and if that one warning isn't heeded, the school authorizes the guards to stop those who would commit violence during a school sanctioned dating event with extreme prejudice. You remember how you moved too fast for the guards to get a good bead on you, how you kept hitting the boy who oozes in the face even as the countless bullets entered you. You wonder how you aren't dead, and one of your tumors says it was because of them you're not dead. You mean that we're not dead, you say. The EMT sitting next to you says *yes, it's a miracle you're not dead*, and you think that living is the worst thing that could happen to you, to the EMT, to everyone else.

The girl with the melting face shakes you awake, you smack your lips, feel the wool from last night's wine swell in your mouth. Your best friend doesn't wait long to start talking about what happened last night on Homecoming. Your eyes open a little more and notice how your best friend's face is melting more than usual, especially around her eyes. *You*

need to come see this, your best friend says, motioning to her computer on her desk. *See what*, you say, and she gestures to her computer again. *Just tell me*, you say, and she gestures to her computer, again. You get yourself upright and hop to the computer. On the screen you see the headline from the school newspaper's website: class president in coma. *Why aren't you celebrating this*, you ask, and your best friend tells you to keep reading. You see six hall monitors were also hospitalized and. You see six hall monitors were also hospitalized and. You rub the sleep out of your eyes to read what's on the screen better. You see six hall monitors were also hospitalized, and the boy who coughs up oil was punished for what he did. The article goes on to say how it took 16 bullets to finally stop the boy who coughs up oil's rampage. Your eyes begin to well with tears and you say over your shoulder, *it looks like the boy who coughs up oil saved us from himself.*

43

You feel your tumors try to move your limbs, try to use your limbs to take the life of the EMT hovering over you, try to use your limbs to take the life of the ambulance driver so they can go back to the cafetorium and finish what they wanted to start, but you've lost too much blood, taken too many bullets for your body to obey their commands. *You knew this would happen, didn't you*, your tumors ask and you nod. You took advantage of their anticipation of the moment they could transform your body into the host of the new American god they've wanted to become from the moment they knew they could alter the chemistry of your body to remake you in their image. If you would have thought about it for too long, the tumors would have figured out how to stop you; beating the boy who oozes nearly to death was a bonus. *You used us*, your tumors say, and you nod again. If you were strong enough, you'd point out how they've been using you, too. The tumors try to move your limbs again, try and use your limbs to take the life of the EMT caring for you, take the life of the ambulance driver, and still, you have lost too much blood, taken too many bullets for your body to obey their commands. *What have you done*, the tumors ask, and you mouth these words so only they can hear them: *the right thing.*

You decide to go home while your mother is at church, praying for whatever she prays to the American god for so you can spend the rest of the day underwater. She stopped taking you to church after your father left you and her for a life better than the one he was a part of. Your mother felt you would curse the congregants, that your presence would anger the American god even more than you've already angered him by driving your father away from your mother's arms, your mother's body. She lets you dive as deep as you want in her wine bottles because she wants you ruined but doesn't have the courage to ruin you with her own hands, which is unlike any of the tenets of the American god in the sense that you are supposed to destroy your own enemies before they destroy you or themselves. You suspect your mother's disobedience of this tenet, her passive-aggressive methodology of punishment is her compromised way of rebelling against the American god that cursed her with a daughter not worthy enough for a father who wants to stick around. The only thing stopping the grief from widening in your chest is that the news article didn't say that the boy who coughs up oil died, only that he was shot 16 times by the guards. For once, you root for the tumors who want to take over his body, who want to become the new American god through a pandemic that they'll spread. You root for them to work their magic and save the boy who coughs up oil's life.

44

The doctor holds up a plastic bag full of bullets coated in black muck as he stands at your bedside. *What's that black stuff around the bullets you removed from my body*, you ask to make conversation, though you already know the answer, and the doctor says, *it was the cancer that metastasized throughout your body*, and you notice the doctor refers to your cancer as "was" instead of "is". *Was*, you ask, and the doctor says, *yes, was, that these bullets, the cleansing fire bestowed upon them by the American god finally eradicated your cancer. Shouldn't you study the cancer to see why these bullets killed it you put me through*, you ask, and the doctor says *no, we don't question the American god's miracles*. You ask the doctor if you can keep the plastic bag full of bullets as a trophy to show his classmates how his body was blessed by the American god, and the doctor says, *sure*, and places the bag on your chest. When the doctor leaves, the black muck forms a face from inside the bag, and says: *we're not finished with you*.

❧

You're not sure why the principal pulled you out in the middle of your American History class. You've been underwater for almost two days, and your memory disconnects from your body now and again. The principal pulls a chair out for you and you're close enough to smell the latest student that the swamp of his body digests. He sees the look of terror on your face and says that you aren't in trouble, and you breathe a sigh of relief. He asks you how well you know the boy who coughs up oil, to be honest with your answer, and you admit going out with him once or twice outside of a school sanctioned dating event. He says breaking the rules is part of growing up, and you again breathe a sigh of relief. He points to a large envelope and asks you to deliver it to the boy who coughs up oil's hospital room. You lean back in your chair, your jaw begins to hang, and before it can hang lower the principal says the boy who coughs up oil survived and is awake and alert and needs to catch up on his homework, how the American god needs him to graduate to serve him on the front lines. The principal smiles: *he's a man purified by the gunfire of the American god.* You agree to give the boy who coughs up oil his homework so you can see for yourself whether the tumors have taken over.

45

You wake up in your hospital bed to see a skeleton that looks like your father. He places his hand on yours and asks how you're doing. You ask him how he's doing instead, and you can tell he lies when he says he's fine, how the tumors in his body are shrinking thanks to the chemotherapy. You were once a skeleton too when your tumors were just ordinary assassins before they gained sentience and figured out that their path to a pandemic, their path to their American godhood was through your body, so they stopped killing you and started altering your body to be their perfect host. You've lived with these tumors for almost ten years, and the doctors refuse to figure out why your tumors refuse to kill you as it would question the miracle of the American god, the miracle of your continued existence. Your father reminds you how the American god has plans for all of us, how the tumors metastasizing throughout his body is part of that plan, seeding his body for what comes next. Your father asks if you need anything from him and you shake your head. The skeleton of your father shuffles off to go back to his room and rest. You turn to the plastic bag of bullets coated in the black muck of your tumors and ask the muck whether this is what they meant by not being done with him, using the skeleton of your father as a bargaining chip.

➤

The girl with the melting face meets you in front of your house, and you ask her if she brought it with her, and she opens her backpack, and you see the glint of a .38 Special at the bottom. She asks you why you couldn't just steal your mother's gun and you say it's one thing in the house that she keeps locked from you. Your mother doesn't trust the underwater version of you ever since that version tried to crack the combination lock of the gun box. You tried your birthday, your mother's birthday, and neither of them worked. You scavenged around the house for your father's birthday or their wedding anniversary and you couldn't find any evidence that he ever existed, not so much to forget the memory of him but to punish you for driving him away with the fusing of your legs, the psoriasis infesting them, your imperfections passing down a death sentence on their marriage. You pull the gun out of your best friend's backpack, inspect it to make sure it's loaded. *You're really gonna do it*, your best friend asks, and you say: *maybe*. The boy who coughs up oil survived being shot 16 times, thanks to his tumors. You want to figure out whether his tumors still have hold over him, stop the pandemic from happening before it can start. You put the gun in your backpack. You tell your best friend you need to be the one who does this, how luck saved the school last time, how it might not save it or her or you again.

46

You come to and see your beloved mermaid standing over you as you lay in your hospital bed. You ask her what she's doing here, and she says the principal asked her to bring you your homework so you can keep up with your classes. You ask her why the principal picked her to do this, and the mermaid says that the principal knows about how close you and her have become, how he's not mad about it, how he said that breaking the rules is part of growing up. You sit up in your hospital bed, stunned that the principal would say something so kind when he typically feeds disobedient students to the swamp of his body, stunned that the mermaid actually said yes to bringing you your homework. The shame of your appearance, of the things you are tethered to grows, so you blush and apologize to her for the way you look, and she places a hand on yours and says, *it's ok*, and keeps her hand on your hand. The mermaid says she needs to know something and your heart races. You calm your nerves and say *sure, what do you want to know?* The mermaid reaches into her backpack and pulls out a .38 Special. She presses the barrel to your forehead and asks whether you are in there. *Yes*, you say, and you look into her eyes to show her they are clear of the influence of your tumors.

❧

Your heart races as you walk past the guards stationed throughout the hospital, past the bustling nurses and doctors treating those that the American god have not blessed with a proper constitution to handle the rigors of life in this (so-called) heaven on earth that the American god has created for us. This is what you hear or read as you walk through the hospital, where the paintings of the perfect, blonde American god stare down at you while he holds the various diseases at gunpoint, his blessed AK-47 gleaming, the child or adult who is open smiling at the American god and his blessed AK-47 as the American god is about to pull the trigger and gun down the disease. The American god allows and encourages the use of guns, allows and encourages the use of guns by the young, but the young may not use them outside of a controlled setting, after school shootings happened daily, and the state said no more. The state needs you to live long enough to become part of the hand of the American god and slay those unworthy to be in the American god's heaven on earth. You reach the hospital room where the boy who coughs up oil stays and you exhale a sigh of relief because he's in a private room, where a mermaid that looks as good as you do can close the door, and no one would raise an eyebrow because the nurses would think you're there to nurse him back to health on your own way (with your hands, with your mouth).

47

The mermaid presses the barrel of the .38 Special deeper into your forehead, your eyes still locked on her eyes. *Are you still in there*, she asks, and you say *yes*. You motion your head towards the plastic bag full of bullets covered in black muck on the table next to the bed. You say the tumors were pulled out with the bullets, how the mermaid can ask them herself. She takes the .38 Special away from your forehead. She picks up the plastic bag full of bullets covered in black muck and asks if what you are saying is true, that the tumors are no longer in him, or at least no longer in control and the black muck forms a y, an e, and an s. The mermaid asks the plastic bag full of bullets covered in black muck how she knows they aren't lying, and puts it to her ear. After a minute, she puts the bag down. You notice the color from her face drain as she drops the .38 Special in her backpack, pulls your homework out of it, and leaves it next to the plastic bag of bullets. The mermaid looks at you for a moment, looks at you like she did on that first date where the possibility of like, of love began between the two of you. She bites her lip. *What did they say*, you ask, and the mermaid stands there for another moment before leaving your hospital room without saying a word.

❧

You press the barrel of the .38 Special deeper into the boy who (maybe, but you're not sure now) coughs up oil's forehead as you look into his eyes to see if the tumors are still there, to see if they will try and take control of his hands to stop you from pulling the trigger, and the boy who coughs up oil looks at you without fear. You think about how the boy who coughs up oil has dealt with death for most of his life, that the gun to his head wouldn't phase him. You watch the boy who coughs up oil motion over to a plastic bag filled with bullets covered in black muck. He says the tumors were pulled out with the bullets and what you hoped was true: his tumors saved his life. You take the .38 Special away from the boy who coughs up oil's forehead, pick up the plastic bag full of bullets covered in black muck. You ask it whether what the boy who coughs up oil says is true, that the tumors are no longer in him, or at least no longer in control, and the black muck forms a y, an e, and an s. You ask the plastic bag full of bullets covered in black muck how do you know they aren't lying. You put the bag to your ear to see if they say anything, and they don't. The color from your face drains as you put the .38 Special back in your backpack and pull the boy who coughs up oil's homework out. You give him the same look you gave him during your first date where the possibility of like, of love began between the two of you. You bite your lip, unsure of what to do. He asks you what the tumors said, and you stand there for another moment before you leave him without saying a word.

48

You regain enough strength to get out of your hospital bed and shuffle into your father's hospital room. You get to his room and see the skeleton of your father sleeping. He stirs when you try to leave and asks if that's you, and you say *yes* because you're not sure he can see you nodding. *What are you doing here*, he asks, and you say you wanted to check on him. *You should get back to your bed*, he says, and you say your cancer is gone. You see him struggle to sit upright in his bed so you help him, fix his pillows to make him more comfortable. *It's really gone*, he asks, and you nod. He holds your hand and says *it's a miracle*, wondering why he didn't think about shooting you with so many bullets at once to cure you. *It's a miracle you weren't killed*, the skeleton of your father says. *Is this girl you like really worth dying for?* You want to keep your father thinking that your tumors were as ordinary as your father's, so you say *yes*, how the class president, the boy who oozes, wanted to build a wall to heaven using boys like you as bricks, that he crossed a line when he started attempting to woo the mermaid with his power. Your father shakes his head, says: *nothing or no one is worth dying for, despite what the voice of the American god might tell you.*

❧

You hand the .38 Special back to your best friend and she notices the gun hasn't been fired. *You couldn't go through with it*, your best friend says, and you say you didn't need to: the tumors said they are gone from his body, she looks at you like you are insane. *The tumors talked directly to you*, your best friend asks, and you nod. You describe the bag full of bullets covered in black muck, how they spelled out 'yes' when you asked whether they were gone from his body. *What about from the hall monitor they hijacked*, your best friend asks, and you were so overwhelmed in the moment of knowing you didn't have to gather the courage needed to end the boy who coughs up oil that you forgot to ask that clarifying question. *What do we do now,* your best friend asks, and all you can think about is opening a bottle of your mother's wine and diving as deep as you can until you find a solution to the possibility of a pandemic or hit the bottom or come up for air, whichever comes first.

49

You wake up to your mother standing next to your hospital bed. *Your father isn't going to make it*, she says, before she leaves your hospital room to be by your father's bedside. You pick up the plastic bag full of bullets covered in black muck, and you ask it whether they (the now removed tumors) could do something to save his father, like talk to his tumors and negotiate a treaty that could keep him alive, and the black muck spells out "no". *Is it because you can't or won't*, you ask the bag and the black muck doesn't respond. Yes, it was your fault that your father was in the hospital when the tumors took control of your body and disarmed your father when he tried to wound you so you could get your tumors looked at in the hospital, but from your intimacy with death, you know it takes a long time for cancer to grow large enough inside a body to be deadly, that your father lied to your mother when he said he saw the doctor for his annual check up. If you had more courage, you would tell your mother not to blame the bullets that allowed the doctor to find your father's cancer.

❧

You catch the acting class president, the boy with flippers for arms, walking down the hall. You stop him and ask if he's heard anything about the class president, the boy who oozes, and he shakes his head. You ask him where his security detail is, and the acting class president says he doesn't need them since he's not interested in building a wall around heaven with defective student bodies. You ask him whether you could get a roster of the security detail so you can interview them about what happened for the school yearbook, and he's taken aback by this request. He reminds you that the school yearbook is for documenting triumph, not tragedy. You remind the acting class president that should the class president die that the yearbook will have to feature his life in it, and the acting class president says the student government spin team will handle crafting that message. *What will you do about the boy who coughs up oil*, you ask, and the acting class president says he won't do anything, how the guards handled the situation appropriately, that he would not want to wage war with any boy who could survive that many bullets. He reminds you though that the boy who oozes may not feel the same, if he ever wakes up, and even if he wakes up, whether his brain is still the same. The warning bell tone pipes through the intercom and you both hurry off to class, and all you can think is *what now, what next?*

50

After the minister finishes the eulogy, he hands you the torch to light the funeral pyre your father has been placed on. It is the American religious tradition for the firstborn son to light his father's funeral pyre when a father does not live long enough to become part of the border wall. You look at the torch and think about how you haven't coughed up anything oily for days, that you can't remember the last time you've felt so alive and full of promise. You at least know now which side of the family you got your cancer from (your father). You look at your father's body on the funeral pyre. His body is covered by the American flag. This is to ensure that the American god recognizes your father as American as the smoke curls up to heaven. You think about whether you should have force fed the bullets covered in the black muck of your tumors to your father, whether the black muck would have smartened up his tumors and kept him alive longer to guide you through your suddenly lengthened life. You expected your father to outlive you, not the other way around. You feel a hand on your shoulder and it's the minister's. He beckons you to send your father to heaven. You gather the strength to say your last goodbye and you light the funeral pyre. The minister asks everyone to come closer to breathe in your father, so everyone can hold onto his memory a little longer, and you breathe him in as he ascends.

We made an offer to our body, the opportunity to be the chrysalis of a new American god, and he refused us constantly. We should not have trusted him when he finally agreed, when we lent him our strength (again) to defeat you once and for all. We promised our body after the bullets (and the parts of us that slowed the bullets down) were removed that we were not finished with him. We know you aren't finished with him. We know how to defeat him once and for all. We know what you want: to curry favor with the American god by building a wall around heaven with the defective parts of the student body, and we can offer you something more. Wouldn't it better to be the new American god than worship him? Wouldn't it be better if you were the wrath and the harvest? Why build a wall around heaven when you could build a tower that you could use to ascend to heaven and claim it as yours? We offer you this in exchange for your unquestioned devotion, your trust and faith in us. We'll even keep the mermaid alive after we defeat our (former) body once and for all, so you can conquer her like you've wanted to conquer her since you first saw her tending the wounded during the war against the tenth graders. This is what we offer. What do you say?

51

You walk down the hall to your locker to a soundtrack of cheers and applause, something you're not used to, something you could never get used to. You wonder what everyone is applauding about. Is it because you were the first student to violate school policy and live to tell about it? Is it because you destroyed the boy who oozes in front of all the other boys and girls gathered at Homecoming? Is it because you dared to defy the principal and the threat of his swamp body devouring anyone who violates school policy? You turn to everyone and bow because it's the polite thing to do. You're too numb to enjoy this adulation. Three days ago, you sent your father to live with the American god. You breathed enough of your father in for him to become a weight in your chest, for him to be an aftertaste in everything you drink or eat. The applause stops when the warning bell tone pipes through the intercom and everyone goes back to doing what they were doing before they saw you, heading off to whatever class they are assigned to for first period. You grab your books for American Science, shut your locker, and head off to class.

The girl with the melting face tells you the boy who coughs up oil is back at school today and says *he looks. Looks like what*, you ask. Your best friend says *he looks. Why are you having a hard time with this*, you ask, and your best friend says that she normally reserves the vocabulary of beauty for girls like you. You stand up and look for the boy who coughs up oil in the cafetorium and you can't find him. *He has to eat lunch in class until he proves he's caught up with his classes*, your best friend says. Your best friend goes on and says she's surprised to see him back at school so quickly. *Because of the bullets*, you ask. *Yes, and because of his father*. Your eyes widen. The boy who coughs up oil didn't say anything about his father when you saw him in the hospital, yet why would've he said anything? You had a gun to his head as you tried to determine whether his tumors still threatened to be a pandemic. Before you can ask what happened or how your best friend knows what happened, she says her father was the minister that oversaw the beginning of the process of sending the boy who coughs up oil's father into the arms of the American god, and you feel the want disguised as a need to find the boy who coughs up oil, to hold him until the levy of his grief breaks.

52

The Sergeant calls you up to the front of the class. He asks that you unbutton your uniform and lift up your undershirt, so you can show the rest of the ROTC cadets where you were shot. You obey rather than take the butt of his rifle to your jaw, and the cadets marvel at the constellation of scars all over your body. *How many times have you been shot*, one of the cadets ask, and you say you've lost count. *This is what someone touched by our American god looks like*, the Sergeant says. *Now, tell us cadet, tell us what happened to you after you were shot 16 goddamn times?* You say you were cured of the cancer that has plagued you since you were 8 and the Sergeant doesn't question how that's possible. He just says: *you are a shining example of what it looks like when our American god touches you with the holy fire of gunpowder.* He puts a hand on your shoulder and says: *even with the threat of death, stuck to your principles and took down someone who was your enemy, that you were willing to die what you were willing to believe in*, and you are stunned that the Sergeant knows that you like the mermaid, and you try not to show it. The Sergeant says: *your survival is proof that our American god forgave you for your transgression against him, that our American god has plans for you.*

❧

Everywhere you walk, girls stop and wait for you to pass them before they start whispering whatever they were whispering before they saw you. You know this pattern of behavior. You have been the match that starts the wildfire of rumor. You have been one of the trees that passes the wildfire of rumor off to the next girl and the next and the next and the next until the boy or girl who the rumor is about burns, starting at the ears, then wherever the rumor decides to roam across the boy or girl's brain or body or both. Your best friend, the girl with the melting face, sees you and she pulls you into a nearby bathroom. She looks underneath the stalls to make sure no one is in them. *What's going on,* you ask, and your best friend says everyone knows about you and the boy who coughs up oil, and you're not surprised that your secret is out. The principal knew about the two of you and didn't threaten to pull you into the swamp of his body for liking or loving someone outside of a school sanctioned dating event, but you also know the principal doesn't spread rumors, unless they serve his interests. *How did it get out,* you ask, and your best friend said that the ROTC Sergeant made the boy who coughs up oil take off his shirt to show the class his bullet wounds, to express the virtues of being baptized and blessed by the American god, and the Sergeant praised him for being willing to die for what he believes in: you.

53

You feel everyone's eyes on you as you walk through the hall. You haven't seen the mermaid since that day in your hospital room, where she held a gun to your head to determine whether you were still you. You know she still has some kind of feelings for you because what girl would sneak a gun into a hospital and be the one to end you unless she wanted to be the one who did it, to look in your eyes one more time, one last time to say goodbye unless she wanted her to be the last thing you see, the last memory you hold as the bullet burrows through skull and brain, the exit wound leaving your last message to the world. The ghost of your father warns you of the impossibility of loving someone in front of an audience, and you agree. You and the mermaid are the latest show for the school. Everyone wants to see what's going to happen next, and you don't want that, and you suspect the mermaid doesn't want that. You ask the ghost of your father what you should do, and he says he's just a memory you've given a voice to, how you already know what to do.

❧

You take the long way everywhere you go just to reduce the chance of running into the boy who coughs up oil in front of the school wide audience now watching every move you make. A couple of times, you almost were late to class, which results in the guards hitting you or firing a shot at your body, one where the bullet grazes you, the wound chiding you for your lack of punctuality until it heals. You like the boy who (does he still?) coughs up oil but not enough to turn your like into a public spectacle, the latest episode in the ongoing opera of high school. The girl with the melting face offers a dangerous solution: kiss her and make the audience go away. Your best friend doesn't care that the guards could kill them for doing that, or the principal does it himself by pulling you and her into the swamp of his body, forced to watch the world disintegrate from the swamp of his body for days, or weeks, or your best friend's father, a minister for the American god, purifying you both in a hail of gunfire to make sure you both are welcomed by the American god in heaven before your bodies fall to the ground. You say to your best friend you need to be patient, to wait for the excitement to die down, to not feed the wildfire of rumor more than it has already been fed. You know there's always a new love, a new tragedy waiting for an audience. You want it to come soon.

54

You remember how your father wooed your mother when you asked him how you were made, before he explained to you the physics and chemistry of how you were made as he was taught by his father (the American god decided your father and your mother were worthy of his intervention and worked in his laboratory to make you worthy enough to grow up and die on behalf of the American god one day). You think of what songs you could stitch together that would convince the mermaid to like you (or, if you're lucky enough, love you) covertly. You stare at the shoeboxes full of the bootleg music your father gave you, your inheritance. You look at the track lists written in his inelegant scrawl. You put one of your textbooks on your lap, lay down a sheet of paper. You chew your eraser as you figure out whether you should let her know (your heaven) that you're miserable now without her company at the beginning or whether yesterday you got so old you felt like you could die because you've been away from her for so long. The ghost of your father shows you the scene from that movie he hated where the boy stood outside, beneath the window of the girl he wanted, and blasted a song that was all about how in her eyes, he could see how he was complete with her, and the ghost reminds you what happened when he tried to do what you're doing now, how his love, your mother, laughed at him into oblivion.

❧

You look outside your window and wonder whether the boy who used to cough up oil will gather the stupid courage of his hormones and do something outside of your window to win you over, to make him worth liking him covertly, and yet you don't want him to be like all the other boys who tried to win your heart, your arms, your mouth through the stupid courage of their hormones, how you'll never feel you're worth dying for or fighting over because you cannot be loved through an exit wound or through the valentine of bruises that your so-called beloved want you to kiss away, as if you could compress them with your lips. You used to think you wanted someone to die for you until they actually did. A death rattle, the clot of his vocabulary, haunts you on nights where it has been days since you dived deep into the ocean of a wine bottle, and your memory clears up enough to remind you of the bodies you've left in the wake of your existence. You think though how, as a mermaid, it's fitting that the desire to confirm or break the myth of your body has left behind a body count; every boy who has ever wanted you thinks of you as a heaven they belong in, that they never knew they were cast out of until they met you. You look outside your window again and the front yard remains absent of the boy who used to cough up oil. You grab the bottle of wine you stole from your mother, open it, and begin to dive.

55

You stare at your half there piecemeal wingman, the project you started to distract the mermaid's best friend, the girl with the melting face, and you wonder what were you thinking, and you know that it wasn't you thinking, it was the werewolf you became beneath the full moon of your hormones. You reach for the half there piecemeal wingman's face to remove it from its half there body, so you can begin to return the parts you stole from where they came from when you hear it say *hello*. You look around the basement, try and figure out whether the voice came from the half there piecemeal wingman's mouth or the ghost of your father you built from your grief, and the piecemeal wingman asks whether you can hear him, and you nod. *You shouldn't have refused us*, the piecemeal wingman says, and you. *You have nothing to say*, the piecemeal wingman says, and you. *We're still here*, the piecemeal wingman says, and you finally gather the words to ask *where*. *You'll see. We could have been the new American god together and now you're going to be one of boys that will become a brick to the tower of heaven that we will ascend to take our rightful kingdom. We promised we weren't finished with you, didn't we?* You pick up the baseball bat and smash the half there piecemeal wingman's face, and from the floor, the scraps cackle at you.

❧

We know you want to wake up from this coma our body put you in, but we cannot let you do that, at least not yet. We must get to know you, our new body, infiltrate your nerves, your muscles, your bones, your blood, your cells. We must know you, our new body, so we are able to mask ourselves if the doctor questions your miraculous awakening from your coma (and they shouldn't as long as you declare how the American god shook you until you finally woke up, how the American god needed you alive and awake to finish building the wall around heaven with the defective parts of the student body as bricks). We feel your hatred, how our presence has made your body defective, too, and we assure you that when we are finished infiltrating your body, you will be strong enough to usurp the old American god and become the new American god and you'll make a tower out of the parts of the student body that are defective to climb, so you can look the old American god in the eye and tell him he is unworthy to live, and you will purify him with his own divine AK-47. Patience, our new body, patience. We will both have what we want soon enough, us the pandemic we need to complete our transformation and your revenge against our former body, your conquest of our former body's object of affection on top of the corpse of our former body, that (damn) mermaid.

56

You stare at the scraps of your piecemeal wingman's pulverized face on the basement floor and wonder whether their cackling comes from what's left of your tumors coursing through your piecemeal wingman or your grief and guilt over your father's death gnawing at your sanity, but that voice coming from the piecemeal wingman is something you're not capable of imagining. You think back to Homecoming, where you charged through the boy who oozes's security detail, how you mounted him and punched his face, punched his face, punched his face, punched his face even as the bullets entered your body, how you couldn't tell whether it was his blood or yours getting into his mouth as you punched his face, punched his face, punched his face, until enough bullets were planted in you to force your fists, your body to stop punching the boy who oozes face. You swallow your panic and think about what your tumors said, how they used the word "brick" to describe bodies, how the tumors talked about building a tower to heaven. You think back to Homecoming again, and you focus on the moment there was blood in the boy who oozes's mouth, and you realize your exit wounds fed the boy who oozes your blood bit by bit, enough for the tumors to infiltrate the boy who oozes's body and rebuild themselves within him. You run upstairs, out of your house. You run and run and run and run and run until you reach the mermaid's house.

You emerge from the ocean of wine you're swimming in long enough to hear something tapping at your window. You look out and you see the boy who no longer coughs up oil standing in your front yard, throwing pebbles at your window. You think for a moment of going back in the ocean, ignore the bombast of his want, but then something hits you: he's not that kind of brave or stupid to try and woo you with something grand. You open the window and ask him what's going on. He says he needs to come in and talk to you, that it's an emergency, and from the ocean of wine, you tell him that his like for you isn't an emergency, how he needs to go back home, and he says (before you can close the window and ignore him) the boy who oozes is alive, and you stop and the ocean of wine begins to drain. *Of course he's alive, he's in a coma,* you say, and the boy who no longer coughs up oil says *no, he's coming back to finish what my tumors started.* You shut the window after he says that. You thought you were rid of the boy who oozes, the tumors threatening their pandemic, to use your high school as a host body for the new American god they want to become. You look out the window again and the boy who no longer coughs up oil stands in your front yard. You make your way out of your bedroom and unlock the front door.

57

You are alone with the mermaid in her house but you hate the circumstances. If your tumors were still in your body, they would demand a thank you for their assistance in getting you into the mermaid's house and would remind you constantly how, if it wasn't for them, you wouldn't have been alone with the mermaid in her house, and they wouldn't let you talk back to them if you tried. The mermaid pours you a cup of wine, asks you to dive to her level so you and her can talk about what to do with the impending return of the boy who oozes, your tumors. You remember the only time you ever tried drinking, and it was when your father let you try a beer while you and him watched baseball. You took a sip and spat it out onto the carpet, and your father didn't get mad at you since you were only five. He said he did the same thing when he tried beer for the first time but got used to the taste. You pick up the cup of wine and down it in a single gulp before you allow yourself to talk yourself out of it. The mermaid picks up to pour you more and you put your hand over your cup; you think you've dived deep enough.

❧

The panic in the boy who used to cough up oil's eyes tells you he's not lying about the impending return of the boy who oozes, his tumors, so you decide that neither you or him should deal with this news sober. You put a cup in front of the boy who used to cough up oil and pour him some of your mother's wine. You tell him to dive to your level, and he stares at the wine in the cup before picking it up and swallowing it all at once. When you try to pour him more wine, he puts his hand over his cup and gives you a wine dark smile. You pour more wine into your cup and dive deeper. You look for the wreckage of solutions to cling to. You could sneak back into the hospital, but you'd need to borrow the gun from your best friend's parents that they didn't know was borrowed. There might be enhanced security around the boy who oozes because of how badly he was beaten, how his parents may not want the boy who used to cough up oil to come finish what he started during Homecoming. You think though there are other ways to finish what the boy who used to cough up oil started, how he doesn't need to be one who does it. You don't care what everyone at the hospital might say about your virtue; virtue is just a way for the American god to control the desire of women.

58

You wake up in the mermaid's bed, your mouth dry, your brain in a decaying orbit you've never felt before. You notice your clothes are still on and the mermaid isn't in bed with you. You see a note on the nightstand, and it says *taking care of our problem*, and the mermaid signed it below. You throw the covers back, start getting out of the mermaid's bed when the door opens, and the mermaid's mother appears, and you both stare at each other, wondering what either of you are doing here. *Where is my daughter,* the mermaid's mother asks, and you shrug your shoulders. You're not sure where she is, or how she's going to take care of the problem that's becoming the boy who oozes, your tumors. *What are you doing here,* she asks, giving you that look mothers give when they want to smite something, and you say you needed to talk to someone about missing your father, and the only person you knew who has experienced that was the mermaid, and the look in the mermaid's mother's eyes softens as she asks what happened to your father, and you tell her half of the truth: his cancer was found too late and he died. Her mother starts crying and she walks over to you and hugs you and you start crying in her arms, as if grief was a levy holding something back, and seeing someone else cry was the crack it needed for you to finally cry too.

❧

You are still drunk enough to not care about how the hospital staff judges you as you walk through the hospital, to the room where the boy who oozes is staying in. You painted your face and dressed yourself up in a way that makes every boy or man look at you twice, the first time not believing a girl likes you exists, and then the second time is to confirm that yes, a girl like you exists. Ambulance after ambulance feeds the aftermath of a twelve car wreck into the emergency room, and you use the chaos to sneak past the guards. You open the door and you see the principal sitting next to the bed where the boy who oozes lays. The principal stands up and asks you what you're doing here, and you didn't expect this. You stammer out something about wanting to check on the boy who oozes, how you wanted to apologize to him for putting him into this situation and see if your voice could be the thing that lures him back to this world and you ask the principal what he's doing there, and he says that the boy who oozes is his son and he gets that look in his eye he gets when he wants to throw a student into the swamp of his body. You leave, keeping your eyes on the boy who oozes and the principal. You run out of the hospital as fast as your fused legs will allow, and you don't stop until the burn in your lungs makes you.

59

You are a quarter of the way to school when the mermaid stops in front of you, hunches over to catch her breath. *What did you do*, you ask, and after she stops hyperventilating, she asks whether you knew that the principal was the boy who oozes's father. You think about when you were eight, when you were friends with the boy who oozes before your tumors marked you defective in his eyes. Before you were marked defective by your tumors, the boy who oozes wasn't oozing then. You think of the principal and rewind the memory of his body whenever you went to the boy who oozes house to hang out with him, and the principal's body was whole when he came into the room to check on the two of you. If you would have known or remembered, you would have told her, you say to the mermaid. The mermaid straightens herself up and says she suspects the principal set the wildfire of rumor about the two of you liking each other to drive a wedge between you and her since the principal couldn't harm you directly, as the guards punished you for violating the no-violence rule during a school sanctioned dating event and you survived their punishment. You now know you and the mermaid may potentially be fighting a war on three fronts: the boy who oozes, the tumors, and the principal, and while the tumors may be in the boy who oozes, they may strike a deal with the principal as well to punish you and the mermaid as they see fit.

❧

You see the boy who used to cough up oil and you stop running as fast as your fused legs would let you when you get close enough to him. You wonder how you or him didn't know that the principal was the boy who oozes's father, whether it was a secret at school. You ask the boy who used to cough up oil whether he knew that the principal was the boy who oozes's father, and it takes him a couple of minutes to remember as the last time he saw the principal act like a father around the boy who oozes was when he and the boy who oozes were still friends eight or so years ago, before the boy oozed, before the principal's body became a swamp he buried disobedient students in. You realize now that the principal didn't seize you, didn't put you in the swamp of his body in his office, in the hospital when you went to the boy who oozes's room to finish what the boy who used to cough up oil started, because the principal has special plans of avenging his son for the two of you, one that moves like a slow knife rather than the cleansing, holy fire of bullets from the American god. You ask the boy who used to cough up oil whether his tumors might reveal themselves to the principal through the boy who oozes and propose an alliance, and he says he wouldn't put it past them. You grab the boy who used to cough up oil's hand and drag him to intercept your best friend, the girl with the melting face, to warn her about what's coming.

60

You cannot believe the mermaid is holding your hand, but the circumstances sour the rush of her skin against yours. An apocalypse is coming because of you, coming for you and the mermaid, with everyone else at school as collateral damage. Your arm hurts as you and the mermaid run hand in hand to intercept her best friend, the girl with the melting face. Your incentive to survive this apocalypse is the mermaid, to be with the mermaid, that surviving something like this together will bring you and her closer, as it has so far, close enough to where she will finally kiss you, kiss you, kiss you. The full moon of your hormones looms over you and you focus on the end of your world, the mermaid's world, to resist its pull. You ask if you and her are almost there, and the mermaid says, *maybe*, her answer ragged. You almost don't want to intercept her best friend so you can keep holding the mermaid's hand. The mermaid stops, and you collide with her, and she says (after catching her breath) she sees her best friend talking to someone in front of the school. You notice the mermaid hasn't let go of your hand when she calls her best friend over to where you two are, and everyone who can see you stops and looks at the two of you holding hands.

We underestimated the mermaid, her blood lust. She didn't have the courage to pull the trigger to eliminate our old body when she thought we were still in him. It would have been easier for us if she did, but we lacked the strength to fool the mermaid into doing it. We don't know what we would have done had your father not been checking on you at that moment. We're not sure how much of your body we've infiltrated yet, and we would have had to reveal ourselves in a place where enough bullets and science could end us once and for all. We feel you want us to reveal ourselves to your father, see if he'll help us become the new American god, help us destroy our old body but we aren't sure whether your father might try to purify your (now) defective body. If you love your father, want us to spare him, say nothing. Keep us secret. Let us give you what you need so you can ravage the mermaid atop the corpse of our old body. The tower to heaven we'll build together can wait a little longer. Patience, mister class president, patience. When we are finally through with you, you will be feared, you will be the alpha and the omega, the blessed AK-47 and the finger that pulls the trigger. Hear that thunder? It's the American god trembling at the thought of us on his doorstep.

61

You ignore everyone staring at you and the mermaid holding hands as you and her talk to the girl with the melting face about the impending return of the boy who oozes and the doom that he'll bring with him. The girl with the melting face suggests going somewhere more private, and the warning bell causes everyone to scatter. The girl with the melting face says she doesn't want to risk being late, that this discussion can wait until after school, and you don't agree with her assessment, but the mermaid says she understands. The mermaid hasn't let go of your hand since she dragged you to her best friend, and you don't want to say anything. *What do we do*, the mermaid asks you, and you tell her that we should spread the word of the class president's return and what's coming with him. The mermaid furrows her brow and says no one will believe that tumors could become sentient and spread like the pandemic in Atlanta that turned it into a necropolis. You tell the mermaid we need to at least try and warn everyone, prepare them, how they might believe you because you are the boy who (everyone else believes) the American god blessed with bullets, cured you of your cancer with gunpowder, how if the American god could do that for you, he could warn you of something that will endanger his beloved children. The final warning bell comes through the intercom, and you and the mermaid let go of each other's hands and run to class.

❧

You didn't realize you were still holding the boy who used to cough up oil's hand until you felt all of those eyes look at you and him and your best friend. You don't know why you didn't let go in that moment, other than to quell the panic coursing through your body. You don't know if the boy who coughs up oil's plan will work. The only science that you and your classmates are allowed to believe in are things that have been handed down by the American god to the teachers who were recorded on VHS passing the knowledge of the American god on to the youth of today. According to the science of the American god, everything good or bad in the world is because of a curse or a blessing from the American god. The boy who used to cough up oil was cursed with cancer, and now he's blessed because the cancer is gone. You are blessed because you are (according to everyone else at school) a landlocked mermaid waiting for the right boy to catch you and love you in the ocean of his arms. The class president, the boy who oozes, is cursed because he was beaten into a coma and will be considered blessed when he returns. You're not sure if your fellow students will heed the boy who used to cough up oil's warnings as they may feel like they deserve whatever is coming.

62

You try and start the wildfire of rumor about the return of the boy who oozes, the doom he'll bring with him in the form of your tumors, and the smoke from the wildfire says something different: you've been made mentally defective by the American god through the cleansing fire of his bullets. Where once your classmates looked at you in awe for surviving 16 bullets, they don't look at you at all, or when they do look at you, they roll their eyes and don't make the effort to even walk past you without lightly body checking you. Maybe the mermaid was right about not warning everyone, or at least in the way that you are warning everyone. One of your classmates, the boy with the hole in his throat, scolds you for not finishing the job during Homecoming. You wonder what it will take for them to believe you before the doom comes for everyone, and you realize the mermaid may have better ideas than you. Based on what you've done, you'll wait until after school to go to the mermaid's house and figure out a plan of action, so she isn't labeled a weirdo or a pariah by being seen with her. You fear by everyone seeing you and her holding hands that the wildfire of rumor will burn her the way it's burned you.

⸙

The wildfire of rumor about the boy who used to cough oil reaches you and you try putting it out by reminding everyone how his father just died, that he's grieving, but you feel the flames starting to reach you. You know based on the whispers that it would be social suicide for you to back up the boy who used to cough up oil, even though what he says about the boy who oozes, and the tumors are true. You tried to warn the boy who used to cough up oil not to spread the warning the way he wanted. He hasn't proven his credibility to the rest of his classmates, even though he survived 16 bullets. Surviving all that gunfire, beating

the (despised) class president into a coma would have been the perfect
foundation to build his popularity from, but an outcast knows nothing
about the social engineering that goes in spreading the wildfire of
rumor until it becomes truth. Now, you go about the dirty business of
disowning any and all (romantic) ties to the boy who used to cough
up oil publicly, saying yes, what he says isn't true, how he feels guilty
about his father's death, how his vocabulary is grief and you are trying
to be a good friend, so he doesn't return himself to the American god
he came from, and the flames start to die down, change direction while
the return of the boy who oozes looms in the back of your mind.

63

You feel two hands on your shoulders during lunch and they belong to
two of the hall monitors monitoring the cafetorium. *You need to come
with us*, one of them says. You don't ask where. The wildfire of rumor
got to the principal, the boy who oozes's father, and now he wants to
have a private conversation with you, maybe bury you in the swamp
of his body, make you watch the world dim and blacken as the swamp
of his body digests your skin, muscle, and bone. You wish your tumors
were still in your body to save you, to beat these hall monitors the way
they helped you beat so many other hall monitors, and in the panic
rising, you stop thinking. You watch the lunch tray go from the table
and into the face of the hall monitor on the right, what's left of your
food flying as the lunch tray connects with his jaw. The hall monitor
on the left pulls out his baton and you watch your foot slam into his
stomach. You watch your fist land an uppercut beneath the left hall
monitor's jaw, his neck snapping back as he stumbles and lands on the
ground. Your ears notice the silence in the cafetorium, and you look up
and notice everyone watching you. You look around, glare at those you
think are looking at you too much, before looking back at the collapsed
hall monitors. You yell: *if the principal wants to see me, he can come fucking
find me.*

You sit stunned during study hall when you find out from the girl
whose mouth opens sideways how the boy who used to cough up oil
beat two hall monitors who tried to take him wherever they wanted
to take him. You used to think that the boy who used to cough up
oil wasn't capable of violence, that it was his tumors who wrote his
history of violence, but the fact he did what he did without his tumors
makes you wonder whether he was like this all along. You ask the girl

whose mouth opens sideways why she's telling you what the boy who used to cough up oil did, and she says how she doesn't know if she could like a boy like that, one who disobeys authority, since the hall monitors are agents of the American god because of their affiliation with the principal. She says she's more concerned about doing right by the American god than giving in to doing what her heart and body want. *He's all yours now*, she says. You realize it would be hypocritical of you to judge the boy who used to cough up oil for doing what he did. You were willing to kill him in the hospital if his tumors still controlled his body. You were willing to kill the boy who oozes in the hospital had the principal not been in there with him, fawning over the comatose monster like a good father should. Maybe (if you survive the impending return of the boy who oozes and the tumors), just maybe, you and the boy who used to cough up oil belong together after all.

64

Two guards walk into your American Algebra class and call your name. Everyone around you moves their desks away just in case you do something stupid, like try to fight them like you fought those hall monitors during lunch; they know your body has an appetite for bullets, and their bodies don't share that same appetite. You stand up a little too fast for the guards's liking and they aim their AK-47s at you. You raise your hands, and say *yes, that's me. The principal wants to see you*, one of the guards says, and they wait or want you to do something stupid so they don't have to deal with the headache you're becoming. You grab your things and walk towards the guards. A guard walks ahead of you out of the classroom, another behind you.

You wonder whether the same thing is going on right now in the class that the mermaid is in, and you hope it isn't. It's not her fault you handled warning the school of the impending threat of the boy who oozes and your tumors so poorly. The guard walking in front of you stops in front of the principal's office and opens the door. His receptionist, the woman with two and a half arms, greets the guard and asks how she can help him. You wonder how long the principal will make you wait to see him, how long he'll allow your fear to rise.

Two guards walk into your American English class and call your name. Everyone around you moves their desks as far away from you as they can to reduce their chances of catching a stray bullet from the guards's AK-47. You stand up, slowly. You put your hands up, slowly. Some guards look for an excuse to execute you instead of doing what they were told. You tell the guards that yes, you're her and you keep your hands up, fighting your nerves from making any sudden movements accidentally. You hop, your pace not too slow, not too fast. One guard walks behind you, the other in front. You do everything you can to not give them an excuse to shoot you. You have a feeling your firefighting efforts against the wildfire of rumor that the boy who used to cough up oil didn't work like how you wanted and now the principal wants to deal with you, maybe use your body as an instrument of psychological torture against the boy who used to cough up oil. You heard once that love is watching someone die, and maybe it is, but you don't want to die in the swamp of the principal's body. You don't want the boy who used to cough oil to die in the swamp of the principal's body. The guard walking in front of you stops in front of the principal's office and opens the door. His receptionist, the woman with two and a half arms greets the guard and asks how she can help him. You see the boy who used to cough up oil waiting. You wonder how long the principal will make you wait to see him, how long he'll allow your fear to rise.

65

You shake yourself out of the quicksand of fear pulling you in to see the guards walking the mermaid into the principal's reception area, likely for the same reason you are here. You wonder whether the principal will force you to watch the swamp of his body digest the mermaid or force the mermaid to watch the swamp of his body digest you.

You reach out to hold the boy who used to cough oil's hand, and the receptionist, the woman with two and a half arms, yells: *no touching.* You pull your hand back. You try leaning in and whisper to the boy who used to cough up oil, and the receptionist yells: *no talking.* You look up at the clock and see only five minutes have passed.

You reach out to hold the mermaid's hand, and before the receptionist can yell at you for touching, you ask her to give you your last wish to see whether what might happen behind the closed doors of the principal's office will actually happen, and she looks at both of you, and the anger melts from her eyes.

You wish it didn't take being on the precipice of death for the boy who used to cough up oil to gather the courage to make the first move. He looks at you and his eyes say how sorry he is for putting you in this situation. You look at him, and you try to make your eyes say: *it's not your fault.* The receptionist picks up the ringing phone, looks at you and the boy who used to cough up oil, looks at the principal's door.

We asked you for patience, to let us fully infiltrate your body, so you could extract your revenge, and we could begin (together) becoming the new American god. We saw what you saw from a host who we have lost control of as we infiltrate you. You may not have the chance to kill our old body, may not have the chance to ravage the mermaid on top of the corpse of our old body because your father may kill them in the swamp of his body before we are finished. No, once you are awake, it will be harder for us to complete the process. We took almost a decade with our old body and while you are comatose, we can accelerate the integration process. Why can't you see the bigger picture? You. Do not open your eyes. Do not move your mouth. Do not say anything. Do not wake up. Do not wake up. Do not wake up. Do not wake. Not wake up. Wake up. Wake. Wake. Wake. What have you done? We don't care if you have done what you feel is the right thing. This is wrong. Doctor, ignore this body. It is still not awake. It is still more coma than boy. Why aren't our words coming out of our new body's mouth? Why can't this doctor hear us? This is not a miracle, we try to say through our body's mouth. Do not call our father, we try to say through our body's mouth. Why isn't any of this working?

66

You and the mermaid hold hands, wait for your sentence, when a phone rings inside the principal's office. You try and listen to what the principal's saying, but he's murmuring. After a minute, his door flings open, and the principal says to his receptionist: *my son is awake and talking. I'm going to the hospital to see him. I'll be back probably in a few days.* He starts running out before the receptionist asks what he should do with the two of you. The principal pauses, glares for a moment at you and the mermaid, glares at you and her holding hands, before turning back to the receptionist: *get a hall monitor to take them back to class.* He runs out, leaves the door open. You and the mermaid look at each other in shock, more about the timing of the boy who oozes waking up, than being spared (for now) from dying in the swamp of the principal's body. The mermaid mouths: *did your tumors do this?* You nod. Your tumors somehow knew you and the mermaid were about to die in the swamp of the principal's body, and rather than allow the principal to end the both of you, they woke up their new body because they want to punish you and the mermaid for your betrayal, for slowing them down from their ascent to American godhood. Your tumors promised they weren't done with you, and now you know they aren't.

A hall monitor walks through the door just after the principal leaves the reception area of his office. The receptionist looks at the hall monitor, says: *how did you know you needed to be here to get these two?* The hall monitor shrugs. *Take them back to their classes,* the receptionist says. She looks at you and the boy who used to cough up oil, and says: *I trust the two of you will tell him where you should be going.* You both nod. The hall monitor gestures to follow him, and you and the boy who coughs up oil do. You follow him to a place where there are no cameras or guards. *Where are we going*, you ask, and the hall monitor stops. He rushes the boy who used to cough up oil, pins him against a row of lockers, and kisses him. You try to pry the hall monitor away from him and he pushes you away. After 10 seconds, he stops kissing the boy who used to cough up oil, and collapses to the floor. The boy who used to cough oil starts coughing that cough he used to have, and coughs up something oily. He looks at you and asks: *do you remember that hall monitor?* You look at the hall monitor and it dawns on you it was the hall monitor his tumors hijacked. You ask the boy who once again coughs oil what's going on, and he says: *the tumors don't have control of the boy who oozes. They need us to stop what they've done.*

67

You slip into the place you and your tumors used to have conversations when you did not want them talking to you through the (no longer) piecemeal wingman's mouth or objects. *What do you mean you don't have control*, you ask.

The tumors, taking the shape and sound of your father, say: *we did not expect our new body to have hate strong enough to overtake us.*

Can we stop him before he can leave the hospital?

We are not strong enough in you to fight through the guards to get to him.

We don't have to go to the hospital. We could try and intercept him at his house.

We are not strong enough in you yet to face him.

How do you get strong enough in me to face him?

Your tumor father puts its hands on your shoulder, looks you in the eye: *where are the bullets we encased to protect you?*

In my bedroom.

You will have to put them back in you. Have the mermaid help you. Go. Now.

You return to the hallway where the hall monitor vomited what tumors he had from your mouth to his. The hall monitor is still passed out, blood seeping from his mouth. The mermaid asks you where you went. *We need to go to my house, now,* you say. You raise your hand and the hall monitor wakes up. He gathers himself, stands upright. *Get us out of here without us being seen*, you say, and you and the mermaid follow the hall monitor puppet.

❧

If you had not seen what the boy who (once again) coughs up oil's tumors could do or would do, you would be panicked right now, almost as panicked as one of those damsels in American fairy tales waiting by a window, watching the horizon for her (declared) dead love to come closer and closer, stained in blood that is his and not his, carrying a trophy to woo the damsel into his arms, and kiss and kiss and kiss as the gunfire from your father salutes him home, your American prince. *What about my best friend*, you ask the boy who (once again) coughs up oil.

The hall monitor puppet says: *we don't need her.*

Yes, we do if you want my help. The hall monitor puppet turns and tries to stare you down with his ink black eyes.

You want my help, you do what she says, the boy who (once again) coughs up oil says. The hall monitor puppet sighs and asks you which way. You and the boy who (once again) coughs up oil follows the hall monitor puppet to your best friend's class (American drama). The hall monitor puppet opens the door, and you see that the class in the middle of a production of the play that celebrates the first time the American god breathed on American soil, blessing Americans with his exhale, blessing them with the privilege of breathing him in. You see your best friend dressed in an American flag baptism dress, which makes you cringe. When a girl is given an American flag baptism dress, she has been chosen as a child bride to the American god and is then set ablaze. This is to keep the American god happy, keep him breathing on America, keep Americans breathing him in.

68

The girl with the melting face won't stop grumbling about being forced to wear the American baptismal dress outside of American drama. *We didn't have time for you to change,* the hall monitor puppet says.

Just keep me away from any open flames, the girl with the melting face says, and she's right about that. American baptismal dresses are designed to attract fire, not slow them down, not stop them. You hear *halt* and you look over your shoulder and see one of the guards walking up to you. The hall monitor puppet stops and you, the mermaid, and the girl with the melting face follow the puppet's lead.

Why are you outside of class, the guard asks, and the hall monitor puppet says: *principal's authorized me to remove them from school for the day.* The guard steps back, aims his AK-47 at the hall monitor puppet. The guard asks the puppet what's the code of the day, and the puppet says *apple pie.* The guard aims at the hall monitor puppet's head. The hall monitor puppet gets on all fours, and you use him as a platform to launch you, and your knees at the guard. You and the guard fall to the floor, with you on top of the guard. You punch the guard in the throat, take his AK-47 from him as he struggles for air, and crack him on the head over and over again until you know he won't get up. You catch your breath, notice the mermaid, her best friend, and the hall monitor puppet stare at you. You drop the AK-47, say: *we need to go. Now.*

❧

You never understood the need or want for violence, the need or want for blood, the need or want to survive. You have always been protected even when you've been threatened, the advantage of your reputation as a mermaid. You thought violence was just one of the American tenets force fed to you once you are old enough to hear the words of the American god and know what they mean. Before everything that has happened, you would have pushed the boy who (once again) coughs up oil away because of what he did to the guard just now, to the hall monitors in the cafetorium. You understand how violence can be hard wired into a boy or girl, no matter how hard they fight the urge. *Was that you or the tumors*, you ask the boy who (once again) coughs up oil as you, him, your best friend, and the hall monitor puppet run as the klaxon goes off indicating a guard has been assaulted and disarmed (!), how the school is on lockdown. Two guards step in front of you, aim, and yell *freeze*, and you watch the boy who (once again) coughs up oil and the hall monitor puppet slide and kick the guards's shins. They don't go down. The guards shove the barrels of their AK-47s in the boy who (once again) coughs up oil and the hall monitor puppet's face. You hear radio chatter going on in one of their helmets. The guards step back, lower their AK-47s. You help the boy who (once again) coughs up oil and the hall monitor puppet to their feet, and run, run, run, out of school, to the boy who (once again) coughs up oil's house.

69

You tell the mermaid, her best friend, and the hall monitor puppet to wait outside while you go in and make sure it's safe, that no one is in there.

You can't face him alone, the hall monitor puppet says.

Is he in there, you ask.

The hall monitor puppet closes his eyes. *Is he in there,* you ask again.

No, we can't feel him. We get glimpses here and there of where he is, how he's feeling.

Stay here anyway, you say.

You unlock the door and find your mother sitting in the living room, staring at an empty wine glass, and your father's gun. She looks up at you, and you notice her eyes are red and wet from crying. She wipes her nose with her forearm, asks: *what are you doing here?*

You cough up something oily in your palm and say you weren't feeling well, so you got a pass to come home early.

School would've called me, your mother says. Her lips thin. *What are you really doing home?* You hear the front door open, and the mermaid walks up next to you and wraps her arm around yours. You make yourself blush, pretend to stammer something about how you and the mermaid snuck out of school to be alone. Your mother looks at you and then at the mermaid and then at you. She picks up the gun and aims it at the mermaid.

Do you love her enough to watch her die?

The boy who coughs up oil steps in front of you without hesitation. *It's me you have a problem with*, he says. *If you're going to shoot someone, shoot me.* The boy who coughs up oil's mother tries adjusting her aim to shoot you, but the boy who coughs up oil keeps moving, mirroring her.

You should suffer the way you made me suffer, his mother yells. *You murdered your father. You murdered the man who loved me, who loved you. You should know what it feels like to watch someone you love die.*

It's our fault he's dead, you hear the hall monitor puppet say as he walks into the living room. He stands next to the boy who coughs up oil, reinforcing the human shield you hide behind.

The boy who coughs up oil's mother looks dumbfounded at the hall monitor puppet: *who are you?*

We are your son's tumors. We did not want the doctor to find out what we were up to so we used your son's arms to take his father's gun away, to shoot him.

The boy who coughs up oil's mother aims at the hall monitor puppet: *why should I believe you?* The hall monitor puppet walks up to her, places the barrel of the gun on his forehead. *We only know how to kill. When our father tumors passed us along into your son, we became smarter, we saw what we could do. Our father tumors grew savage, ravaged your husband. The bullet did not kill him; it allowed.*

Your ears ring after his mother pulls the trigger, after the bullet explodes from the back of the hall monitor puppet's head.

70

You watch the hall monitor puppet get up from the ground, the hole in his head dripping. Your mother stands stunned long enough for you to get the gun out of her hand. You open the chamber, empty it, the bullets falling to the carpet. Your mother looks at you: *what?*

You need to go lie down, you say, and your mother nods and shuffles off to her bedroom. *Are you still in there*, you ask, your tumors piloting the bleeding hall monitor puppet.

I'm coming for you, the puppet says in a voice that isn't his. *Say what you need to say to the old American god because tomorrow, your reckoning comes.* The bleeding hall monitor puppet looks at the mermaid: *you can either be my queen in the new American heaven I'll build or you can be a brick in the tower that leads to my new American heaven.* The bleeding hall monitor puppet looks down before it looks back up. *It's worse than I thought*, the bleeding hall monitor puppet says.

Could the boy who oozes control me, you ask.

He could try, but you've fought us longer and harder. We will stay down here though so he cannot see through our eyes what you are doing. Go. Take as much of us back as you can, quickly.

You look at the mermaid and the girl with the melting face. *Stay here,* you say. You run upstairs, into your bedroom. You open the plastic bag of bullets covered in black muck, swallow each one, licking the black muck from your fingers.

❧

Father, there is something I need to show you, we hear our new host body say. He extends his oozing arm and makes us stop it oozing.

His father looks at his solid arm, says: *it's a miracle from the American god.*

Look what else I can do, we hear our new host body say. He flicks his hand and makes us form needles that fly out of his fingertips.

His father looks at the needles quivering in the wall before looking at our new host body, says: *it's a miracle from the American god. My boy has been blessed with gifts that will serve him.*

I don't want to serve the American god. I want to be the new American god, our new host body says, and his father takes a step back, eyes wide, teeth gritted. He grabs the boy who oozes and drowns him in the swamp of his body, says: *I cannot have a blasphemer for a son.* Our new host body pulls himself out of the swamp of his father's body, brushes his father's muck away.

You have two choices, father: help me ascend or become a brick in the tower that leads to my new American heaven.

His father takes the family AK-47 off the wall, fires the entire magazine into our new host body. The boy who oozes makes us close the exit wounds, knit his insides back together. *You chose poorly,* our new host body says. He makes us turn his hand into a knife, and we watch him stab his father in his stomach. *There is still a use for you.*

7**1**

You feel the tumors multiply throughout your body after you swallow the muck covered bullets. The tumors urge you to sleep and you obey, for once. Your tumor father emerges from the mist of your dreams, says, *we must ready your body for what's coming.* Your tumor father shows you the boy who oozes stabbing his father with his hand knife.

How will we prepare the mermaid and her best friend?

This is your fight and your fight alone.

You ask your tumor father: *how well do you know the boy who oozes?* And you know what their answer will be before your tumor father opens their mouth: not well. Your body remembers the tumors, the control they had over your muscles and nerves, bone and skin.

You've always been wired for violence, your tumor father says. *To survive this, you'll need to embrace what you've denied.* Your tumor father shows you the boy who oozes throwing needles from his fingertips. *He uses us in ways we did not expect.*

Then we will need the mermaid and her best friend's help, you say, and your tumor father sighs. You hear the hall monitor puppet tell the mermaid and her best friend to come up to your bedroom. *We will need to ask their permission first, give them the choice you never gave me,* you say, and your tumor father grunts, hating how much you are right, hating how they need you more than you need them.

❥

You and your best friend see the boy who coughs up oil twitching on the floor. You go to try to make him stop twitching, and the bleeding hall monitor puppet says *don't*. The boy who coughs up oil stops twitching and gets himself to his feet. You notice the plastic bag that held the bullets covered in black muck is stained and empty.

We need your help, the boy who coughs up oil says.

Both of us, your best friend asks, and he nods.

What will it take, you ask.

You'll need to also be a host for my tumors.

Will it be permanent, your best friend asks.

I'm not sure. This is a lot to ask from the both of you. Only together can we stop what the boy who oozes has become.

You look at your best friend, and her eyes say: *let's do it. Okay*, you say. The boy who oozes cups your chin and kisses you, slow and deep, and you feel a firework show go off throughout your body as he kisses you. As he keeps kissing you, your fused legs stop being fused, the persistent itch and burn of your psoriasis disappears. When he stops kissing you, you fall to the floor. You ask the boy who coughs up oil for scissors, and you cut your pants enough for you to walk with your (now) unfused legs.

We've made you better, you hear the tumors say, using your father's voice.

72

You feel the firework show going off throughout your body as you kiss the mermaid, as your tumors migrate copies of themselves from your mouth and into her body. This is not how you wanted to kiss the mermaid for the first time. You wanted to earn your way into her heart, into her arms, not through an impending threat but with classic (bloodless) romance. You wanted to win her over with mixtapes and poems, through grand, yet thoughtful gestures, but death seems to get in the way of everything you want to do. *You should be thanking us*, your tumors say, not in the voice of your father, but in their normal hiss. They only use your father's voice to comfort you, to teach you, to give you good advice. Though they need you to stop the mistake they've made, they are still willing to cut you to remind you of what they are, to remind you of what you are to them: a meat puppet. This time though, you pull the strings. You will fight the boy who oozes on your terms, with the mermaid and the girl with the melting face working with you. You suspect to stop the boy who oozes, you'll have to die but before you die, you'll need to make sure the tumors won't live on in the mermaid and the girl with the melting face. You'll need to make sure your tumors no longer have a body that they can try and use to become the new American god. *What are you thinking*, your tumors ask, and you ask: *you don't know?*

Your best friend looks at you and her eyes say: *my turn*. You know she's been wanting to kiss you since the first time her body soured at the idea of boys, their clumsy hands, their sweat and smell.

She isn't strong enough to transfer copies, the boy who coughs up oil says.

Arms akimbo, the girl with the melting face says: *you just don't want me kissing who you hope to be your future girlfriend.*

He's right, the bleeding hall monitor yells up the stairs. *We are strongest in him because we have lived in him for years. We left behind enough material to make ourselves whole in him. We are getting to know the mermaid as fast as we can, so she is ready for what all of you will face.*

The girl with the melting face huffs, closes her eyes: *let's get this over with.*

You watch the boy who coughs up oil walk up to her. He closes his eyes, maybe pretending it's you he's kissing again. They kiss like they are drowning and need air, her face dripping on him, hoping to choke him with her skin, like she has done so many other times boys kissed her and she wanted them to stop. The boy who coughs up oil finally breaks away, and your best friend collapses. You try to see if she's ok, but the boy who coughs up oil stops you: *let them do their job.* You and him watch your best friend twitch and spasm on the floor, her melting face slowing to a trickle, until her face becomes solid for the first time.

73

You cough up the skin that the girl with the melting face tried to choke you with as you kissed her, as copies of your tumors traveled up your throat and down hers. You wipe away her dripped skin from your face. *We are making them better*, your tumors hiss. *Can't you see how we can make you better too?*

You know your tumors are making the mermaid and the girl with the melting face what they think are their perfect selves, the landlocked mermaid now able to walk like a normal girl, the girl with the melting face no longer melting, her cheeks now something most boys would dream of caressing if her cheeks wanted boys to touch them. Even as your tumors need you to help correct their mistake, they are looking for new ways to betray you, new meat puppets who will do what they are told willingly as long as the meat puppets look like (what the tumors think) are perfect versions of themselves. You're not concerned about the mermaid agreeing to use her improved body to betray you. She knows what your tumors are capable of. The girl with the no longer melting face though you're not sure you can trust. She sees you as an obstacle to the mermaid's arms, the mermaid's heart.

You're not sure how you feel about your (now) unfused legs. You feel like the tumors have taken away your mythology, made you ordinary. You try and will your legs to fuse again, and the tumors ask: *why be what you were when we can help you become what you should have always been?*

You know not to trust these tumors, even as they (supposedly) fix your body, make you strong enough to fight the boy who oozes. You trust the boy who coughs up oil though, and you trust he has a plan to stop the tumors from taking over your body and your best friend's body, stop them from making you and her into a vessel for the tumors for their ascent to American godhood.

You were never fine as you were, your tumors say, and you say to the boy who coughs up oil that your tumors are talking to you, and they are trying to get you to believe who you were before them was imperfect. You ask him how you handled the seeds of doubt they kept planting in him for all the years the tumors lived in him. He whispers in your ear: *hush*, and you stop hearing the hiss of your tumors.

They won't be in you long enough for you to learn to block them out, the boy who coughs up says.

Your best friend, the girl with the (no longer) melting face wakes up. She feels her smooth, solid face. She runs to the bathroom, probably to marvel at her non-melting face.

74

You slip into the place where you can talk to your tumors, and you ask them: *why didn't you try to make me a perfect version of myself?*

Your tumors, taking the shape and sound of your father reply: *you believed us a thing that would kill you, so we pretended to be a thing that could kill you, except when your life was threatened, until you asked us to take control of your body when you were losing sleep trying to build that piecemeal wingman of yours to distract the mermaid's best friend to better woo the mermaid, only for the mistake we made to help do that for you.*

You punch the father tumor in its mouth and its head snaps back, black blood flying out of its mouth. The father tumor rubs its jaw: *we admit we deserved that.* The father tumor looks into your eyes, and you feel it trying to crowbar its way into your intentions. Black blood begins trickling from its nose. You say: *try all you want but you're not getting in.* You want to say how this will be the last time you and the tumors will coexist, how you will end this to stop their madness, their march onwards becoming the new American god, a gloating promise. Your father tumor gives up breaching your intention, asks: *we need to get the mermaid and her best friend up to speed with our abilities. Where do you suggest we go?*

❧

You and your best friend, the girl with the (no longer) melting face, follow the boy who coughs up oil. Your best friend can't stop touching her smooth cheeks, her no longer melting skin. You were surprised when the boy who coughs up oil told the bleeding hall monitor to stay behind. *Don't we need him to help us train,* you asked.

The boy who coughs up oil shook his head, said: *the boy who oozes is able to hack into the hall monitor. He must not see what we are up to.*

Your eyes widen as the abandoned auto factory grows closer, the place where you and the boy who coughs up oil went on your first and second date. *Won't the jobless fathers be drinking here, pretending to go to work,* you ask.

The boy who coughs up oil nods, says: *we're gonna send them back to their families. We're going to beat the truth of what they really are into them.*

You hear the crack of knuckles and you see your best friend intertwining her fingers, flexing them, working out the kinks in her bones. You're not sure you want to do this, and the tumors, in the voice of your father, ask: *why not?*

Because my father might be in that building, you say aloud.

75

While you loved your father, his memory is a weight that needs to be lifted for you to stop the boy who oozes from using his tumors from becoming the new American god, building a tower to his so-called heaven with the bodies of your classmates. Your father did everything he could to stop you from becoming like him: baptized by the American god through the blood of his enemies. He taught you how to fight, but only to defend yourself. He taught you not to kill, unless your life is threatened. He taught you to earn love, not take it.

Do you have to do this, your father tumor asks, and you say, *yes*. You need to lift the weight of your father to become him, the savage, relentless killer. *We could do this for you*, your father tumor says, and you say, *no*. You suspect the moment you give your tumors control that after they correct their mistake, they will use you, the mermaid, and the girl with the (no longer) melting face to return to their agenda of becoming the new American god.

You put your hand on the mermaid's shoulder, ask: *your father left you, didn't he?* The mermaid nods. You look at the girl with the (no longer) melting face, ask: *if your father knew the truth about you, he would cleanse you with the holy fire of bullets, right?* The girl with the (no longer) melting face nods. You say: *let's baptize ourselves for battle by beating the truth into these jobless fathers so we can let the weight of our fathers go.*

❧

We jump when the boy who oozes kicks the door down, the corpse puppet of his father looming behind him. *Where are they*, he asks. He looks into our eyes, tries to crowbar out the whereabouts of our original host, the mermaid, and her best friend, and he can get nothing from us because we did not hear or see what they were planning. We see blood trickle from his nose as he keeps trying to get into our memories. The boy who oozes punches us in the stomach and we cough up some of the blood this body has left, asks us again: *where are they?*

We don't know.

He bends down, looks into our eyes: *I forgive you for your betrayal for without you, I would not be the American god I have always wanted to be.*

We straighten ourselves. The hole in this body's head isn't weeping as much. We've finally stemmed the bleeding.

The boy who oozes says: *I will lure them out and punish them for their sins in the way I punished my father for his sins.*

Before we can ask how, the boy who oozes grabs us and throws us in the swamp of the corpse puppet of his father's body.

76

The jobless fathers are drunk, as usual. The jobless fathers also have their guns on them, as required by the American god. The mermaid and her best friend take shelter behind a wall as you brawl with the jobless fathers. The one you're fighting goes down after a jobless father accidentally shoots him. *You need to trust your tumors*, you yell, before a bullet strikes your collarbone. Before you can take down the jobless father who shot you, the mermaid emerges from cover. She zigzags, stays low, as the jobless father's aim is dizzy with drink. She lands an uppercut that snaps his head and body back, sending him to the floor. The other jobless fathers stop doing what they're doing, pull out their guns, and aim at you and the mermaid. *A little help here*, you yell. You hear a loud crack and one of the jobless fathers collapses, the girl with the (no longer) melting face standing over this fallen jobless father. Some of the jobless fathers start aiming at the girl with the (no longer) melting face. You clench your fists, say: *go home while you can still walk and tell the truth to your families of your joblessness, and pray to your American god for his forgiveness for your laziness.* The jobless fathers look at each other, then look at you, the mermaid, and the girl with the (no longer) melting face, laugh, and aim for your heads.

❧

The jobless fathers who are drunk and panicked scurry away after you beat six of them in a matter of minutes. The jobless fathers who can still walk under their own power help the jobless fathers whose legs or arms are broken out of the abandoned auto factory. You know that they will probably lie, say they were hurt at work, and that lie will hold until the bellies of their wives and children grumble waiting for their disability checks. You catch your breath, wipe the sweat from your brow, the blood from the corner of your mouth. *How are we doing this*, you ask the boy who coughs up oil, and he says the tumors have his father's muscle memory. You notice the boy who coughs up oil's shoulder bleeds from a bullet wound, and he says he's fine. *It doesn't look like it*, you say, and his body corrects you as the bleeding stops, the wound closes. *Will we be able to do that, too*, you ask, and he says he's not sure so let him be the one who does something stupid. Your best friend looks at the American flag baptismal dress she's still wearing, how it's stained with the blood of the jobless fathers she beat truth and shame into. *Can we go to my place so I can get out of this thing*, she asks. The boy who coughs up oil closes his eyes, says: *we need to stay here for the night.* You ask your tumors why you have to stay here, and they refuse to answer. You ask the boy who coughs up oil why they have to stay here, and he refuses to answer, too.

77

You get glimpses of the bleeding hall monitor drowning in the swamp of the principal corpse puppet. Through the muck of the bleeding hall monitor's eyes, the last thing you see is the boy who oozes heading up to your mother's bedroom. The last thing you hear from the bleeding hall monitor is a gurgle of *don't*. You're not sure if you should tell the truth on why the mermaid and her best friend can't go home. The boy who oozes will use the mermaid's mother, her best friend's parents as bait to lure them out when they are not yet strong enough to face him. The girl with the (no longer) melting face tries to leave and you get in her way. *You can't leave*, you say.

The girl with the (no longer) melting face throws punch after punch, and you're able to dodge left, right, keeping arms behind your back. *Why can't we leave*, the girl with the (no longer) melting face yells.

Tell them, your tumors hiss. *They need to know what they will lose.*

Your tumors are right. You need them to trust you, you need to trust them. You let the girl with the (no longer) melting face punch your jaw once before you tell them what you saw through the bleeding hall monitor's eyes, how the boy who oozes threw him in the swamp of the principal corpse puppet, then went upstairs to kill your mother.

You and your best friend, look at each other for a moment thinking about the possibility of your mother and her parents being killed by the boy who oozes, and you two start laughing. Your mother has never forgiven you for your body betraying you, for fusing your legs and riddling them with psoriasis. She has allowed you to kill yourself slowly, never counting the wine bottles you stole, always making sure there were wine bottles in the cupboard for you to steal. She is the reason you kept yourself underwater, to ignore the poison of her indifference. Your best friend's parents preach the word of the American god. Your best friend's parents tried bleeding her love of girls like you out of her through thoughtful bullet wounds. Your best friend's love is a threat to the purity of the faith that her parents preach. You and your best friend laugh because you and her know that the boy who oozes will do the two of you a favor. If he only knew it would be better to leave them alive, to align with them, to use them to torture you and her. You look over to the boy who coughs up oil, and you stop laughing when you see the grief spread across his face, his eyes becoming wet. You and your best friend wish you knew what it was like to have parents who you'd miss when they're gone.

78

You go to the place where you can talk to your tumors, and before your father tumor can say anything, you punch it in the stomach, then grab its ears and knee it in the face. The father tumor turns over, puts its hands in front, begs you to stop. *You killed my father and mother*, you yell before you kick it in the jaw. Your tumor father coughs black blood. When it gets on all fours trying to stand, you kick it in the stomach again. Your father tumor flips over on its back, coughs more black blood.

We could have saved your mother and father if you would have worked with us, the father tumor hisses.

Saved them so you could enslave them in your ascension to American godhood, you ask, then kick your father tumor in its ribs. You feel the place where you can talk to your tumors shake and shake. The ceiling crumbles, a piece crushing your father tumor. You come back to the abandoned auto factory, back to the mermaid shaking your shoulders.

They're coming closer, the mermaid says. *Can't you hear the helicopters?*

You listen to the helicopters swarming the area. You killed a guard, took two others out. They hunt for you and your accomplices. They will shoot you on sight if you are caught.

What do we do, the girl with the (no longer) melting face asks. Your body says run, but your tumors say hide.

❥

You hear the helicopters swarming around the area looking for you, your best friend, and the boy who coughs up oil. The boy who coughs up oil brought everyone here so your (new) tumors could get to know your body, so everyone could get to know what their bodies are now capable of. The boy who coughs up oil doesn't feel anyone here is ready to fight the boy who oozes, but you wonder why the three of you have to fight him alone, why not have the guards hunting you hunt him as well, see the abomination that he's become?

Whose house would the boy who oozes go to last, you ask.

The grief and panic on the boy who coughs up oil's face becomes a question: *why?*

We need to lure the guards who are hunting us there

My body can handle the bullets. Yours may not.

We have to try.

The boy who coughs up oil closes his eyes, probably going to the place he goes to when he talks to his tumors for advice. He opens his eyes, says: *your house would be the last place he likely goes to lure us out, saving your mother for last out of some twisted chivalry, out of his want for you.* You cringe at the thought of having to save your mother, the woman who blames you for your father leaving, for your body betraying you.

79

You're stunned at the idea of going to the mermaid's house, to lure the guards hunting the three of you down into also firing on the boy who oozes.

Don't do this, your tumors hiss. *They aren't ready.*

The mermaid has earned your trust, breaking you out of the prison that your tumors put you in when they had you yoked to their whims, becoming a host for copies of your tumors to help you correct the mistake your tumors made in bargaining with the boy who oozes to start the pandemic that would turn them into the new American god they've wanted to become.

How far is your house from here, you ask the mermaid.

A mile.

You close your eyes, picture the geography of how you would get there, whether you can weave in and out through alleyways and buildings to obscure the view of the wake of helicopters hunting for the three of you. *How fast can we run*, you ask your tumors. After a minute, you don't hear an answer, so you ask your tumors again. After a minute, you don't hear an answer, so you are about to ask again when they finally answer: *you would sacrifice our ability to protect you, to protect them. There are limits of what we can do.*

What's going on, the mermaid asks you. You laugh and say, they're concerned for our safety, and you know the truth: they're concerned you'll all die before they get a second chance at becoming the new American god.

Your copies of the boy who coughs up oil's tumors panic at the thought of the wake of helicopters sending the three of you into the arms of the American god they want to replace. *Should we split up and then meet at my house to make it harder for them to catch us,* you ask.

That's a bad idea, your tumors say, and you hush them.

The boy who coughs up oil nods, says: *take the way that gives you the most cover.*

Your tumors have made you and your best friend stronger and faster, but they may not have had enough time to vaccinate you against bullets.

Are you sure that's a good idea, your best friend asks the boy who coughs up oil.

No, but we could use all the help we can get. The boy who coughs up oil crouches in a sprinting start position: *wait five minutes and then go. See you soon.* The boy who coughs up oil takes off faster than you've seen anyone run before.

Your best friend crosses her arms, says: *you're going to get us killed.*

Would it make you feel better if we left together? Your best friend thinks about it and shakes her head. You try to figure out how many minutes it has been since the boy who coughs up oil left as the sound from the wake of helicopters grows distant.

80

You hear the wake of helicopters follow you as you sprint to the mermaid's house. *Stop or else*, one of the helicopters says. You don't think about why they're warning you rather than shooting first, and then asking your dead body rhetorical questions. You're concentrating on pushing your tumors to push your body to its limits. You've never used them to run this fast, where everything blurs. A bullet lands in front of you, and you zig and keep running. A bullet lands in front of you again, and you zag and keep running. A helicopter hovers low enough to try and block you, the door gunner aiming at you and you leap through the helicopter's open center, keep running. The sound of the wake of helicopters becomes more distant as you get closer to the mermaid's house. You slip into the place where you can talk to your tumors, leaving your body on autopilot. *How are you*, you ask your father tumor, and it looks ragged, bleeding.

Why do you care, it says, then coughs up something oily.

Need to make sure we can keep going at this pace.

Your father tumor winces, replies: *we hope the boy who oozes isn't at the mermaid's house. We need time to recover.*

You snap back when you hear something fast flying behind you. You peek over your shoulder and see a small missile stalking you. You stop, turn, and face the missile.

What are you doing, your tumors hiss, and just before the missile hits, you turn and run again, and you hear the explosion, the shockwave barely touching you.

❧

You, your best friend, and the boy who coughs up oil arrive at the same time at your house. The wake of helicopters hover over your house. *On your knees or else*, one of the helicopters yells. You look to the boy who coughs up oil for guidance, and he's exhausted from pushing his tumors to the limit. His eyes say: *we're finished.* You, your best friend, and the boy who coughs up oil get on your knees. The wake of helicopters still hover though, and you see your front door open and from it emerges the principal. He walks over to the three of you, then looks up at the helicopters, and then waves his arms. The wake of helicopters ascends and then flies away. The principal crouches down, cups your chin, says: *we still have uses for my father.* Before you can say anything, the principal pulls you into the swamp of his body. You watch from the muck coating your eyes your best friend try to run, only for the principal's arm to transform into a tentacle, coil around her, and then drag her into the swamp of his body. The boy who coughs up oil gets up, throws a leaping punch, but his fist gets stuck and the swamp of the principal's body sucks him into the muck. *I'm not done with you*, the muck says.

81

The principal's body is more ocean than swamp. You tread in him, waiting for the boy who oozes to do whatever he has planned to do with you, the mermaid, and her best friend. The bones of various disobedient students float by you as your tumors fend off the muck from getting in your mouth, your nose, your eyes, in your lungs. You look through the muck for the mermaid and her best friend, and all you see is muck.

What you did was foolish, your tumors hiss. *The mermaid lured all of us to our doom.*

You see a pencil float by and grab it. You touch the tip and it feels sharp enough. You try to stab yourself in the arm, try to open yourself enough for your tumors to sneak out through your blood and gain control over the boy who oozes, but the muck stops your hand in mid stab. The muck thickens around your arms, legs, and body, holds you still. The muck leaves your head intact so you can breathe. You suck in some of the muck, and you choke on the taste of it. You hold the muck in your throat for as long as you can.

What are you doing, your tumors hiss, and you cough the muck up as hard as you can.

❧

The muck caresses your thigh. The muck caresses your arm and shoulders. The muck asks you to want him, to love him, to be his right hand in the new American heaven he plans to build, to want him, to love him. You say no, and the muck says if you don't want him, don't love him, then he will strip your best friend of her skin, muscle, and bone, leave her corpse floating in the swamp of this body. You call his bluff, and say you would rather die than want him, love him, be his right hand in the new American heaven he plans to build, and you feel the muck coil around your body, squeeze your arms, legs, chest, and neck. You start to black out from the pressure until you feel something warm coursing through your body, and the muck stops trying to crush you. It locks your body where it is. *Are you ok*, your tumors ask, and you nod as best as you can. The muck clears up enough where you see the front doors of your high school coming closer and closer. The corpse puppet principal talks to one of the guards, and you make out the words coming out of its mouth: mandatory emergency assembly. You offer to trade your want for him, your love for him, for the lives of the entire school, and the muck laughs at your sudden selflessness.

82

You hear the murmur of the students gathered in the cafetorium by gunpoint through the muck of the corpse puppet principal's body. You see through the muck how the guards stand in front of each possible exit to ensure every student stays in the cafetorium while the principal addresses them during this mandatory emergency assembly. You get a look through the principal's eyes how bored and frustrated everyone in the cafetorium is, and the guards don't need to correct this behavior, just make sure they stay seated until the announcement is over. You were able to cough up some of your own tumors to see if they could spy on what the boy who oozes is doing, see if they could hijack this corpse puppet you, the mermaid, and her best friend are trapped in. The principal steps up to the microphone set up in the middle of the cafetorium, taps it once or twice, and the feedback makes everyone wince. The principal clears his throat, says: *ladies and gentlemen, thank you all so much for being here with me today. I know it's late and you want to go home. This won't take long.* He extends his arms and a stream of muck seals the front doors. The guards start firing and the muck slows down the bullets. A stream of muck seals the emergency exits. The guards keep firing their AK-47s at the principal. When the clips hit the floor, the principal extends his fingers, and shards of muck fly out. All the guards fall to the floor, bleeding and begging for their lives.

❧

The muck lets you watch the students trample the fallen guards as they beat their fists against the muck covered doors, stick their hands through the muck and try to open the muck covered doors, try everything they can to escape. The ROTC students pick up the AK-47s that the guards dropped, ready them to fire.

You cannot kill the American god with the gift he gave you to slay his enemies, the corpse puppet principal bellows. *Put them down and you will be forgiven my children.*

Our American god is beautiful and perfect. He uses his blessed AK-47 to smite his enemies, our enemies, one of the ROTC students says. *Fire!* They fire their AK-47s at the principal, and the swamp of his body catches the bullets, then spits them out.

Do you see now I am your American god, the corpse puppet principal says as the ROTC students search the guards for more ammunition.

You say: *you will have what you want from me if you stop this.*

Do you promise, the muck says.

Yes.

The muck carries you out of the swamp of the principal's body, licks you clean of whatever muck is left. The ROTC students stop reloading when they see you, two-legged and beautiful. The students who aren't beating down the doors stop to look at you, two-legged and beautiful. *Follow him and we will live in the American heaven we deserve,* you say. You hear something wet come out of the principal's body, and it's the boy who oozes walking over to stand at your side. He says: *I am here to show you what paradise will be like as your new American god. Join me or become a brick in the tower to heaven.*

83

You see through the corpse puppet principal's eyes the mermaid standing beside the boy who oozes, surveying the cafetorium. The ROTC students still hold onto their AK-47s like security blankets. You trust whatever promise the mermaid made to stop the corpse puppet principal from attacking the students trapped in the cafetorium is hollow. You watch her kiss the boy who oozes's cheek, and it makes you cringe almost as much as the mermaid is probably cringing right now.

The son is now the father, and the father will become the new American god if you believe in me, the boy who oozes says.

One of the ROTC students stops cowering and starts firing. The corpse puppet principal bends itself into a circle, surrounding the boy who oozes and the mermaid. A spike of muck emerges from the corpse puppet principal, impales the ROTC student who fired on it. The corpse puppet principal returns to its original form. The other ROTC students look down at their fallen classmate, then look at the mermaid and the boy who oozes. They throw down their AK-47s, put their hands up, beg for forgiveness, their lives.

We almost have you free, your tumors hiss.

What about the girl with the no longer melting face, you ask.

You first. Then we will free her. We will need you to distract him while we free her. We need more of us in this body.

You inhale the muck, hold it in your throat, and cough until you feel your throat bleed.

❧

The taste of the boy who oozes's skin haunts you. You want to rinse out the taste with your mother's wine, dive as deep as you can to forget your mouth ever touched his skin. You shake your disgust out of you and pretend to fawn over the boy who oozes as the corpse puppet principal looms behind you. He cups your chin, looks into your eyes, and asks: *darling, which one of these boys should be the next brick in the tower to heaven?* He points at the other ROTC students frozen in fear. You walk over to the ROTC students, pretend to inspect them for their level of heresy committed against the boy who oozes.

Keep him distracted, your tumors hiss.

You look over at the boy who oozes, say: *forgive them. You are a new god to them. They are used to the old American god and were only defending him. You'll worship this one now, right?* The ROTC students nod. The boy who oozes pauses for a moment, before summoning the corpse puppet principal to absorb them one by one.

The boy who oozes says: *if they reach American heaven, then they will know they have been forgiven.*

The double doors sealed by muck explode. Your ears ring and you choke on the smell of charred flesh. Guards pour through the opening and start shooting every student in the cafetorium. The corpse puppet principal attacks each guard, stabbing them or drowning them with the swamp of its body.

84

We need to disarm the guards and keep them alive, you say to your tumors.

No.

The boy who oozes commands the corpse puppet principal to kill the guards who are trying to kill the students as part of the quarantine protocol. The American god believes in cauterizing disease with the holy fire of bullets. If bullets cannot cauterize the disease, then the agents of the American god will send something more. If the guards die, the more will come. Better to destroy a building and everyone inside it rather than let the inhabitants spread whatever they are infected with. It's for the greater good, you and your kindergarten classmates were told during the lecture about preventing illness by washing your hands and praying to the American god. You swim in a direction that makes sense. The swamp of the corpse puppet principal's body tries to slow you down, but the tumors you hacked and wheezed into the swamp prevent it. You emerge from the swamp of the principal's body and charge at the nearest (living) guard. You kick the guard in the stomach, take his AK-47 out of his hands, and crack him in the back of the head twice to make sure he's dazed, not dead. You shoot the legs out of the other (living) guards, disarm them as they writhe and bleed on the floor.

How dare you interfere with the plans of your new American god, the boy who oozes yells, then commands the corpse puppet principal to kill you once and for all.

> ❧

Your elbow splashes in the boy who oozes's jaw, making the corpse puppet principal go limp. The boy who oozes rubs his jaw. His brow ripples in fury. He puts his hand around your throat, lifts you high, says: *how dare you touch the American god in the way you have touched him. Soon, you'll find out whether you will be forgiven.* You strike his wrist as hard as you and he makes his arm liquid, releasing you from his grip. As you gasp for air, the boy who oozes stands over you. *I should have expected this from you,* the boy who oozes says. *No more bargaining with your body, with your love. I do not need your love or your body. The American god can pick and choose from his disciples who will sit at his right hand.* You watch his hand turn into a knife. You kick him in the shin as hard as you can, but your foot just goes right through it, the muck of him sticking to you. He laughs until something hits him hard in the back. He turns and you see a glimpse of what looks like a muck creature punching the boy who oozes in the face, sending him reeling. The muck creature follows up with a roundhouse kick, and the boy who oozes spins and falls to the floor. The muck creature walks over to you, helps you up. It wipes its face and you see your best friend's eyes.

85

You look over at the swamp monster standing over the boy who oozes, and you recognize the voice of the girl with the no longer melting face when she coughs, sputtering the muck of the corpse puppet principal's body out of her throat. The surviving students flee through the hole that used to be the front doors of the cafetorium. The boy who oozes gets to his feet and tries to command the corpse puppet principal to stop the fleeing students, but the corpse puppet principal won't move from where it stands, won't chase after the survivors. You squat next to one of the guards you shot, ask him whether the school is locked down. He nods. You ask whether he can deactivate the lockdown, and he shakes his head. *How long do we have*, you ask, and the guard won't say. You look over at the mermaid and her best friend, say: *you need to get everyone out of here. You need to get them as far away from here as possible.* The boy who oozes charges at you, his fingers now claws. You use his momentum against him and throw him across the cafetorium. His body crashes into the bleachers. You look over, and the mermaid and her best friend stand still watching you. You walk over to the mermaid and kiss her long and deep, kiss her like you may never see her again because you're not sure you'll see her again. You press your forehead against hers, tell her to save as many people as she can, how you'll correct the mistake your tumors made.

❧

For the first time, your heart breaks over the honest heroism in the boy who coughs up oil. Every boy before him who tried to be noble was for the purpose of winning you over, not to actually be noble. Your best friend taps you on the shoulder, bringing you back from the preemptive grief spreading in your chest. *There's still more guards,* she says. *They're going to gun down everyone.* You look at the boy who coughs up oil as he walks over to the boy who oozes splayed out in the bleachers. Your best friend tugs your arm, starts dragging you away. You keep telling yourself over and over again that this isn't a goodbye, that this can't be the end. *You need to snap out of whatever's going on if you want to live through this*, your best friend says. You shake her grip and begin running alongside of her, into the thicket of panic and bullets. You channel your anger and grief, and knock out the first guard you see in a single punch, shattering the faceplate of his helmet. You toss the guard's AK-47 to your best friend and she cracks another guard in the jaw with the butt of it. Whatever guards are left swarm to you and your best friend's location. You and her face a wall of AK-47s aimed at you. You and your best friend put your hands up, listen for any more gunfire, and neither of you hear any. Whatever guards are left are focused on the two of you, not on any of the other students.

86

You walk over to the boy who oozes splayed out in the bleachers you threw him in to after he tried rushing you, tried to gouge you with his claws. You pick him up by the collar and his collar melts in your hand. You see the boy who oozes willing a spike to emerge from his stomach, and you punch him in the face to make him stop, and the spike recedes. He looks over at the corpse puppet principal that was his father as if he's trying to will it to stop you, and you slap him in the face to make him look at you instead.

You do not do this to an American god, he says, coughs up something black and bloody.

You say: *you killed your father, made him a monster. You've scared away everyone who followed you before you became this. For the first time in your life, you're alone.*

The boy who oozes looks over at the corpse puppet principal, tries to not be alone, but it doesn't respond. You pick him up and throw him to the middle of the cafetorium floor. You step down from the bleachers, walk over to the boy who oozes as he coughs something black and bloody, gathering air.

Get up, you say. *We fight one-on-one for the first time ever. No crowd to cheer us on. No one to step in and save you.* You step back, give the boy who oozes space to get to his feet, put up his fists.

❥

The boy who coughs up oil used to be my friend until I caught him coughing up something oily in the bathroom in third grade. His oily phlegm was a sign that he was cursed by the American god, and I had to cleanse our school of his corruption. I tried so many times, first with my fists, then with my friends, then with my power as class president, and I could not smite this boy. Even after the bullets that went through the boy who coughs up oil as he beat me during Homecoming blessed me with these gifts, I still cannot smite this boy. I try to will the body of my father to protect me, to fight for me, and the body of my father will not listen. The American god is trying to punish me for my attempt to usurp him and his American heaven, and that's fine. Blood is the mortar that binds the bodies I need to build the tower to heaven, where I will finally meet the old American god and throw him out of a heaven that belongs to me. I get on my feet. I try to remember what my father taught me about fighting, before I figured out how to get others to fight for me. I spit in the boy who coughs up oil's face, blitz him as he reacts. When I'm finished, he will be the first brick in my tower to heaven.

87

The boy who oozes spits something black and bloody at your face as he tries to rush you, but you just step aside, elbow him between his shoulder blades when he intersects with where you stood. The boy who oozes goes down and you give him space to get up, to put up his fists.

You are toying with him, your tumors hiss, and you disagree. You want the boy who oozes to know what it's like to lose in a fair fight, to feel the weight in the ethics of this kind of losing. The boy who oozes finally gets up, spits something black and bloody on the floor, then takes a wild swing at you. You sidestep his desperate punch, and hit him in the face, drops of his oozy skin flying. You felt something crack against your fist, probably the jawbone beneath all that ooze. You want to say something pithy, ask him now that you know he has bones, where his spine is, but your fists and feet want to do all the talking, and they are. The boy who oozes reaches out for the corpse puppet principal, and you hear him beg for it to move, to deal with you, and it just stands still.

The boy who oozes looks up at the ceiling, screams: *I am supposed to be the new American god*, before he collapses to the ground, crying and bleeding. You look over and the corpse puppet principal begins to move towards the both of you.

❧

You remember the story your father read from the American bible how the American god captured heaven and made it American heaven, how (with the help of his gold AK-47) he gunned down each angel who attempted to attack him with their swords, how he shot the old god in the kneecaps to remind him only cowards kneel and ask for help, how he listened to the old god beg for his life for 13 days before shooting him 50 times, one bullet for each of the states he would look down upon from American heaven, one bullet for each state he would bless with his divine presence, the gun smoke starting the foundation of the holy exhale from the American god once he took his place on his new throne. You remind yourself as you cry and bleed how the American god's journey wasn't easy, how he sold off his wife and child to obtain his gold AK-47, how when he came back down from heaven to finally rescue them, they were desiccated corpses. You get to your feet slowly. You wobble and sway as you put up your fists, spit something black and bloody on the cafetorium floor. You say: *you, agent of the old American god, shall be smited by my own hand*, and the boy who coughs up oil looks at you, and laughs and laughs and laughs and laughs until the corpse of your father comes closer and closer to the two of you. You look up to the ceiling, say: *your reign will be over soon.*

88

You and your best friend catch your breath after beating and disarming the last of the guards in the school. You try not to look at the students that they've killed as part of the quarantine protocols, try to not look to figure out whether any of the bullet riddled bodies used to be someone they knew, or liked, or hated. You hear the clamor of the survivors as they try to open the front doors, try to break windows to escape through, and the doors won't give, and the chairs bounce off the interior blast shields covering the windows. You hear an explosion and screaming, smell cooked flesh, and still the survivors panic.

You crouch down next to a guard that's still conscious, and ask: *how do we deactivate the security system?*

You can't. It won't shut off until you and all of your classmates are dead.

You slap the guard in the face, say: *there has to be an override*, and he says *there isn't an override for quarantine protocols.*

Your best friend asks the guard what happens if all the guards die, and he says: *the site gets cauterized.* You ask what he means by that, and the guard says: *the site and everything in a one-mile radius gets cauterized to prevent whatever's happening from spreading.* The guard peels back his wrist, reveals a timer ticking down from 47:02. *If you're all not dead before this timer hits zero, we're all getting cauterized.*

❧

You've been in love with the mermaid since the first grade, when you did not know what that kind of love meant, even when you knew how that kind of love could kill you if your parents found out, your father a preacher promoting the word of the American god. When you finally gathered the courage to confess your feelings to the mermaid, she hugged you and told you she loved you, but not the way you wanted her to love you. The mermaid promised to keep your secret, and she has. You look at the timer ticking down, now 46:01, and you try not to think about the love you'll never have, try to focus on the need to stop this cauterization from happening.

We need to go to the principal's office, you say.

That won't stop anything, the guard says. *Either all of you die or we all die.* From all of your father's preaching, you have been told over and over again that the needs of the American god outweigh the needs of the many or the few.

Why the principal's office, the mermaid asks.

There might be a way to call off whatever's coming.

You grab the mermaid's hand and begin running to the principal's office. You run and run and run and run as hard as you can. For the first time in your life, knowing your father's words may save your life and the mermaid's.

89

You and your best friend get to the principal's office and the two of you see some of the surviving students gathered outside of it, trying to break through the blast door. They must have the same idea your best friend has to see if there's something in the principal's office that could stop the cauterization from happening. Your best friend burrows through them and notices the palm reader next to the principal's door. She burrows back through to you.

We need your boyfriend to lure the principal over here, your best friend says.

He's not my boyfriend, you say, and she gives you that *yeah, sure he isn't* smirk she gives you when she calls you out on a lie but you're telling the truth. You care whether he lives and he's a pretty good kisser, but this attraction you feel towards the boy who coughs up oil is tainted by the possibility of his death. Part of you wants to use your body to say goodbye to him if the cauterization can't be stopped, if the two of you might die in each other's arms, but that's not necessarily like or love or lust. You know fear is the worst way to start a relationship from how your mother chose your father, her fear of dying alone, and despite that choice, she still died alone at the hands of the boy who oozes. You tell your best friend to stay there while you go back to the boy who coughs up oil, ask him to lure the corpse puppet principal here, and you run back to where this nightmare continues.

❧

You run after the mermaid to make sure she isn't going to do something stupid in coaxing the boy who coughs up oil to lead the corpse puppet principal to its office. You stop next to her as she stands frozen in the entrance of the cafetorium.

What's wrong, you ask, and she points, and you see the corpse puppet principal impaling the boy who oozes and holding the boy who oozes high so his body can slide down the spike that is now the corpse puppet principal's left arm. The boy who oozes screams and cries and bleeds, and demands why his father's body will not obey him.

We could have worked together, the corpse puppet principal says. *We could have worked together and become the new American god, but you betrayed me. We would have built that tower to heaven. We would have given you the mermaid as your trophy.* The corpse puppet principal throws the boy who oozes across the cafetorium. It turns and looms over the boy who coughs up oil, says: *we promised we were not done with you.* The corpse puppet principal arms become tentacles, lash out to grab as many corpses as it can, and use the corpses to make itself taller, wider, and thicker. The corpse puppet principal is now a corpse golem. It looks over at the two of you and sprays something black and sticky, and you grab the mermaid and leap out of the way as the black goo seals what used to be the cafetorium's front door.

90

The corpse puppet principal looms over you with its newly gathered corpse skin. You should have known your tumors would do something like this when you coughed them into the swamp of the corpse puppet principal's body while you were trapped in it. The corpse skin has made the corpse puppet principal taller, thicker, wider. You charge at the left shin, channel your tumors to make you faster and stronger, and all you can take off is two, maybe three bodies off. The corpse puppet principal laughs through its corpse skin mouth, hiss: *is that the best you can do?* You channel your tumors and you charge again at the wounded shin, taking off another two to three bodies. The corpse puppet principal starts teetering until it sheds all of the corpse skin from its legs. The corpse puppet principal raises its arms, and the shed corpse skin gets on their feet and shuffles towards you, the mermaid, and her best friend. The corpse puppet principal and its (newly shed) shambling corpse skin all say together: *we're not finished with you*, and you know better to fight through the corpse skin to get to the corpse puppet principal. You need to focus on getting through the remaining corpse skin protecting the corpse puppet principal and finish your treacherous tumors once and for all.

❧

You run over to where one of the guards lays bleeding. You roll back his sleeve and see 38:01 ticking down. You wonder whether the tumors can reactivate the corpse principal puppet's memories and see that cauterization is coming for all of them unless it escapes from the school. You want to warn the boy who coughs up oil about impending cauterization but you don't want to tip off the tumors piloting the corpse puppet principal, to have it focus on escaping and begin its pandemic towards American godhood. You grab the remaining ammo clips from the fallen guard. You pick up two AK-47s, hand one to your best friend. You and her load your AK-47s.

We need to get out of here, your best friend says.

We need to stop that, you say, motioning at the corpse puppet principal and its remaining corpse skin, the shed corpse skin shambling to do whatever it is the tumors want them to do.

What are we shooting at, your best friend asks, and you fire upon the shambling corpse skin, the bullets sending the corpse skin back to the cafetorium floor they were taken from. Some of them still shamble towards you, the bullets to their body not enough to stop them. The remaining corpse skin focuses on encircling you. You see through the cracks the forming corpse wall that your best friend runs over to you, wielding her AK-47 like a club.

91

You bounce off the corpse skin surrounding the corpse principal puppet's chest and land on your hands and feet. The corpse puppet principal takes a swing, and you clipped by its corpse knuckles as you dodge. Your shoulder throbs. You rotate your arm, try to work the pain out.

The corpse puppet principal laughs at you through its corpse mouth. *We could have been the new American god*, it hisses, *but you decided your love for that mermaid is more important. At least you can die knowing that your worst enemy died before you.*

You look over to where the corpse puppet principal threw the boy who oozes, and you can still hear him breathing. You summon what's left in your tumors and leap over to the boy who oozes. You land next to him and you see the hole in his stomach closing, his black blood pooling beneath him.

What do you want, he coughs.

Your help.

He spits something black and bloody in your face, asks: *why should I help an agent of the old American god?*

We won't survive if you don't. Don't you want to be the one who kills me?

The boy who oozes looks at you and nods: *what must I do?*

You kiss him, siphon some of his tumors to mingle with yours, and the pain in your shoulder goes away. When you finish kissing the boy who oozes, you look at each other horrified. You feel stronger, but you don't know how much longer you can last.

You and your best friend catch your breath after beating the shed corpse skin until they stopped moving. You look at your shirt, your arms, and notice how blood-soaked you are. You look at your best friend, and she's also blood-soaked. You would kill something alive for your mother's wine right now, to dive into that ocean and not come up until morning. You finally focus your attention on the corpse puppet principal laughing through its corpse mouth at the boy who coughs up oil. The boy who coughs up oil is where the boy who oozes lays bleeding, probably mustering the strength to attack the corpse puppet principal. You start channeling your tumors to the boy until your best friend says: *stop. There's a better way.* She walks over to the fallen guard and drags his body over to you. You see 31:01 ticking down on the timer strapped to his wrist. Your best friend puts her finger on the guard's neck: *he's still alive.*

What does that have to do with anything?

Your best friend chokes the life remaining out of the guard. *When a guard dies during quarantine, it sets off a timed trigger in their body armor. We have about a minute before he explodes.* You help her lift the guard's body, count to 50 mississippi before throwing the guard grenade at the corpse puppet principal.

92

The guard's body that the mermaid and her best friend threw explodes just before it hits the corpse puppet principal, and it's not a normal explosion. The liquid fire from the guard's exploding body splashes all over the corpse puppet principal's new corpse skin. You've never heard your tumors scream like that before, even when you quadrupled your dosage of your daily medicine. You gag at the smell of burnt flesh and boiling blood. The corpse puppet principal sheds its burning corpse skin. It sprays black goo all over the burning corpse skin to get it to stop burning. You channel your remaining strength and sprint across the cafetorium and dive into the swamp of the corpse puppet principal's body before it realizes what you're doing. You feel the muck try to reject you, but your body prevents it. You feel the corpse puppet principal's hands reach for you, and you tell its fingers to go away, and they do.

You cannot do this, the muck hisses. *You cannot stop us.*

You tear open your wrist with your teeth, use your blood to connect your body with the corpse puppet principal, with the tumors who have betrayed you again and again. You go to the place where you've talked to your tumors before, but in this corpse puppet principal instead.

This will end here, the room says, and you nod.

❧

You want to follow the boy who coughs up oil into the swamp of the corpse puppet principal's body, but your best friend stops you.

We need to get into the principal's office to stop the cauterization from happening, she says.

Before you can ask how she strangles another fallen guard, and you and her throw the body at the black goo sealing the hole that used to be the front doors of the cafetorium. The liquid fire from the explosion eats through the hole, starts working its way up the walls. You wait for the sprinkler system to kick in, but it doesn't.

Quarantine protocol shuts off the sprinkler system, your best friend says.

The corpse puppet principal sprays black goo from its hands to put out the fire. It says: *go now*. The voice isn't the tumors but the boy who coughs up oil. Whatever he's doing in the swamp of the corpse puppet principal's body, it's working. Your best friend grabs your hand and pulls you away from the twitch and sway of the corpse puppet principal's body, the stench of burnt flesh and boiling blood.

Do you really need to keep killing the guards, you ask your best friend.

Yeah. They chose to be the hand of the American god, to be the ones who punished us for whatever rules they thought we broke. We didn't have a choice on whether we got to believe in him.

93

Your tumors take on the form of your father and they grow this form four times larger than you remember him, the room adjusting for this form's height. Your tumors think they're getting into your head by trying to beat you down in the form of your father, but you don't think twice when you jump kick this father figure's right knee, and the father figure buckles and gets on bended knee. You throw a leaping uppercut and the father figure shrinks to a size more comparable to how big your father was while he was alive. Your tumors punch and punch and punch and punch and punch and punch and you match each punch with a block, block until your tumors make a mistake, or get exhausted from punching you. *We will not be stopped*, your tumors yell, and they throw punches even faster. It finally lands one and you fly across the room and slam into the wall. Your tumors sprint to continue punching you, and you duck just before it lands the next punch, and you punch the father figure in the stomach, knocking the air out of it. You get behind the heaving father figure and snap its neck. The father figure collapses, then melts, then takes the shape of a mucky version of the mermaid before the tumors you gave her unfused her legs. You punch the muck mermaid in the face and it reels back. It catches itself from falling and spits something black out of its mouth at your feet.

❧

You and your best friend drag over a guard in front of the blast door protecting the principal's office. She picks up one of the AK-47s from the floor, checks the clip to make sure there are any bullets in it, then fires it at the two guards. She yells at everyone still around you to take cover, and you and her make everyone run as fast and as far away as they can. You cover your ears as you run, and that doesn't help a lot when the bodies explode. You and your best friend run back and see the smoking hole that used to be the blast door, and you and her see another blast door sealing the principal's inner office, this one thicker than all of the other ones. The fire behind you starts to spread and you and her get out of the principal's outer office. You and your best friend stare at the growing inferno. *What do we do now,* you ask. Your best friend looks at the timer she lifted from the guard and you see it ticking down from 19:11. You suggest trying to find more guards to stack, to use to blow a hole through a wall or the front door, and your best friend shakes her head, says: *we need your boyfriend to fix this.*

94

The muck mermaid fixes its face, looks at you like you dared to do what you just did, punching it in the jaw, and you say: *you're not really her. You're not really my father or whatever other forms you decide to take.* The muck mermaid raises its arms and a cage emerges beneath your feet, trapping you. The cage shrinks, trying to crush you. You close your eyes, tell the cage to go away, and it disintegrates. The muck mermaid turns its arms into tentacles, wraps them around you, lifts you high trying to squeeze the life out of this version of you. You tell the room to sever the tentacles, and the room cleaves them off of you. The muck mermaid looks at you with something that resembles shock.

This is our body, the muck mermaid says. *We will rid ourselves of you.*

You feel yourself starting to weaken. You flash over to your body suspended in the middle of the swamp of the corpse puppet principal, and you've lost more blood than you expected from the right wrist you tore open with your teeth. You go back to the room where you and the muck mermaid face each other. You will the room to bring the muck mermaid over. You will your mouth to open wider than it ever has before, and you start digesting the muck mermaid. The muck mermaid tries to turn into a shape that can escape your grip, but you tell the room: *don't let it.*

❥

We feel our old host's body dying within our new body, and yet we cannot stop him in this place. Our new body will not listen to us, will not fill his lungs with our swamp, will not drown him, will not break his bones, will not eat through his skin. We try to fight our old host for devouring us, our identity, but our new body will not help us.

We remember when we were dumb, when all we wanted was to just
hollow out the interior of our host body, and turn what we cleared
into a suburbia, but then the American god touched us and made us
realize we could do so much more. We beg and plead with our new
body to let us continue our work, beg and plead with our old host's
throat and stomach to let us continue our work, but we are losing
ourselves, the memory of how we made our old host's muscles sing,
how we tinkered with our old host's nervous system, how we cheered
when he made the boy who oozes bleed for the first time with our help,
how we beamed with pride as he trusted us to pilot his body when he
could no longer be awake while he worked on his convoluted scheme to
build a piecemeal wingman to distract the mermaid's best friend, how
he trusted us to infect the mermaid and her best friend with copies of
us. We tried talking to our copies, to see if they would listen to us, to
use the mermaid and her best friend to help us, but even those copies
of us stopped listening.

95

The room where you devoured your tumors shakes, debris from the ceiling falling around you. You tell the room to put you and the remaining half of the muck mermaid dangling from your mouth in a bubble, and it does. You go back to the version of you floating in the swamp of the corpse puppet principal's body and you see the actual mermaid trying to shake you awake. You tell the swamp of the corpse puppet principal's body to hold her still so you can concentrate, and it does. You have the swamp of your new body release her after a minute and write this question: *what's going on?*

The mermaid shows you a timer ticking down from 10:39, and says: *we can't get out. My best friend can't get in the principal's office in time to try and cancel the cauterization. Whatever you're doing, hurry.*

You have the swamp of your new body pull the mermaid close to your soon-to-be old body, and you kiss her in a way that says goodbye. You kiss her in a way that wishes you and her had more time to be normal teenagers orbiting around each other, until your courage or her courage decayed the orbit enough to draw the two of you into each other's arms. You kiss her in a way that shows her what you would wear at prom, what song you would have used to dance with her in her driveway when you took her home, the one where the sea stole the only girl he loved. You would have whispered in her ear after the song finished how she was just like heaven.

❧

You feel the boy who coughs up oil go limp while you're in his arms. You look down and notice the last dribbles of blood leaving his torn open right wrist. You feel the grief, the anger, start to swell in your chest, rush to your fists and teeth until the swamp of the corpse puppet principal's body says: *it's ok*, and it sounds like the boy who coughs up oil.

What did you do, you ask.

They're gone. They're finally gone.

What did you do?

I ate them. This body is no longer theirs and that body (the swamp gestures to the body of the boy who coughs up oil) *is no longer here.*

The timer is now at 8:02 and ticking down. *What now?*

Purge you of your tumors, then purge your best friend of her tumors, and then save as many of the survivors as we can.

You feel the swamp brace you as it reaches down your throat, fills your lungs, your blood. You struggle and gag and panic. You feel your legs fuse back together, your psoriasis returning. You cough up something murky and bloody, and the swamp apologizes: *this was the only way. Get everyone into the cafetorium or as close to the cafetorium as you can.* You reach for the timer and swamp says: *leave it. Need to know how much time is left.* The swamp opens up to lead you back to the cafetorium, back to the burnt bodies and boiled blood, back to the infectious panic.

96

You look around, listen for the hiss of your tumors in this room where you used to talk to your tumors. You search yourself, listen for the hiss of your tumors, and all you hear in this room, in yourself is silence. You finally defeated your tumors once and for all but at the cost of your mother, your father, the mermaid's mother, the girl with the (soon to be again melting face), the boy who oozes's father (whose body is now your body), the students who didn't survive the first and second wave of the guards trying to cleanse the school of you and your tumors, of anyone who came in contact with you and your tumors, of everyone within a mile of this school when the cauterization comes. You shake yourself out of counting body after body after body after body when the timer the mermaid left behind inside you says: five minutes. You command your new body to stretch. You command your new body to be a flood, a raging river, an ocean. You hear the last of your father's voice saying he's proud you are doing the right thing. You hear the last of your mother's voice saying she's sorry, how your father's death wasn't your fault. You hope they are looking down on you from wherever they are as your body stretches and stretches and stretches, filling the cafetorium with the swamp of you. You ask the American god to put you in a heaven where you can live the life you would have lived with the mermaid as if all of this never happened.

❦

Your best friend stares at you as you hobble over to where she is, and you forget you are still covered in the muck of the boy who coughs up oil's new body. You say: *get everyone you can into the cafetorium. Now.* You can tell your best friend wants to ask questions, like why are you covered in the muck of the boy who coughs up oil's new body, why are your legs fused again and riddled with psoriasis, but there's maybe three or four minutes left before the cauterization comes. Your best friend runs and yells for everyone to follow her to the cafetorium, to spread the word, and your best friend grabs you as you, her, and everyone else in earshot joins you in this stampede. Everyone stops at the hole that used to be the front doors of the cafetorium when they see it flooding with black muck. One of the students says: *I'd rather be cauterized than drown.* Some of the other students in the stopped stampede nod.

It's safe in there, you say. *It's the only way we're going to survive.* You and your best friend don't wait to dive into the flood that the boy who coughs up oil's body. You both swim as far and as deep as you can, not looking back to see whether anyone else jumped in. You get their hesitance; they feel safer in the arms of the American god than this murky unknown.

97

You feel the strain of flooding the cafetorium with your body. You see 1:39 on the timer and will yourself to hold it together a little longer. *Where am I,* you hear someone ask, and you see it's the boy who oozes, the wound where your tumors used this body to impale him finally closed.

Shelter, you say.

The boy who oozes pauses after he hears your voice, asks: *why didn't you let me die? Why did you save me?*

You remember before the tumors manifested how you and the boy who oozes were best friends, how you had each other's backs in elementary school when the bigger kids bullied you, how you would pretend to sleep long enough to talk to each other at night via walkie-talkie about your imaginary friends, about what you wanted to be when you grew up (he wanted to be an astronaut and claim the moon to be New Florida, and you being good with math back then wanted to be an accountant with superpowers fighting the forces of Neo-Liberalism). Your tumors erased your friendship because of the American god's teachings that the boy who oozes's father beat into him nightly: you deserve what you get. Tumors are evil, are death, making you evil, making you death.

It wasn't your fault you became what you are, you say. *Your father molded you to what he wanted you to be, and you didn't know any better.* You see the boy who oozes start to cry, start to realize what he's done. Despite everything that's happened between you two, you want him to survive this.

❧

You watch your best friend choke and writhe as the swamp of the boy who coughs up oil's body fills her lungs, enters her eyes. Your best friend tries to fight this, tries to resist, and the swamp feels this and apologies, says: *this must be done.* The swamp leaves your best friend's body and she coughs up something black and bloody, and her face begins to drip, drip, drip, drip, drip, drip again. You see her skin drip into her palms and she starts crying. You swim over to her, hug her, tell her everything is going to be ok, and she says: *it's not. How could he do this to me? How could he give me back this face?* You remind her that your legs are fused again, too, and riddled with psoriasis like before, and she said: *that just makes you the mermaid you've always been.* You know why the boy who coughs up oil did this, removed his tumor copies from you and your best friend, how there can't be any copies of his tumors if he wants to make sure the tumors can't come back, can't survive the cauterization. The swamp tells you and your best friend to sleep, and you try and fight it, try to fight the heaviness in your eyes. Your best friend gives in and you keep trying not to. *You don't want to be awake for this,* the swamp says, before the swamp begins to shake. You get caught up in the thrash of the swamp as it says goodbye.

98

The mermaid tells you what it's like to swim, what life beneath the ocean is like, and she says it's not as exciting as the life of someone as landlocked as you leads. You reach across to hold her hand and she doesn't stop you. *How much time do we have before you have to go back to the ocean,* you ask, and she shrugs, says: *whenever you have to go home.* You and the mermaid lay on the roof of your high school and connect the stars into shapes you've always wanted them to connect as. She draws a heart and you draw an arrow, and she asks what that means, and you tell her that you are falling more and more and more for her every day and the arrow is your feelings wanting to burrow through her heart so she can fall for you more and more and more and more every day. The mermaid rolls over to her side to look at you better, tells you she doesn't need an arrow burrowing through her heart to fall more and more and more and more for you. She caresses your cheek and says she already has. You close in for a kiss, and she closes in to kiss you, too. You kiss and kiss and kiss and kiss and kiss and kiss. You breathe through your nose so you don't have to stop kissing her and as you kiss, you swear the night sky flashed white for a moment or two, the stars coming back into focus.

❧

You thrash through the swamp of the boy who coughs up oil's body when whatever is used for cauterization hits the school. You feel the swamp's temperature rising. You can make out through the murk something bright and orange, trying, eat through the boy who coughs up oil's body. *Are you ok,* you ask the swamp, and the swamp says nothing. Whatever the boy who coughs up oil is doing is working as that something bright and orange dims, then fades. You ask again if the swamp is ok, and it doesn't answer. You look over at your best friend and you see she's still asleep. Whatever the swamp did to put her to sleep worked. *How long are we gonna be in here for*, you ask, and the swamp doesn't answer. You give up asking the swamp questions and try to put yourself to sleep like you should have when the swamp asked you to, but you can't sleep; your anxiety electrifies your body. You swim around to see if anyone else made it into the swamp and you see the boy who oozes, also sleeping the way you wish you could sleep right now. You're surprised the boy who coughs up oil saved him, even after everything the boy who oozes put him through, put you through. *Not much longer*, the swamp finally answers your last question, but still won't answer the first question you've asked twice: *are you ok?* The swamp instead asks you whether you're ok, and you're not sure how to answer.

99

The mermaid hovers over you, clasps your hand as you lie in the hospital bed. The doctor says something about the American god, about him blessing you with the long life you have, how you should let go and finally be by his side, and you disagree. If you had it your way, the mermaid would be in this bed instead and you would be holding her hand. You would be bearing the weight that grief brings as you watch her die, but she's watching you die, she's bearing the weight that grief brings, and you see it starting from her eyes. You apologize for not being able to give her the children she wanted, your cancer robbing you of that, and she hushes you, says that life with you was still good regardless of the children you couldn't have. You start crying and it makes the mermaid cry. She is the only reason why you aren't dead, why you won't let go, and you tell your body to sit up, to hold her one more time, to kiss her like you've kissed her these last 30 years, and your body won't listen. The mermaid kisses your cheek, whispers in your ear: *it's ok for you to let go.* You think about how you met, how you and her fought to stay together, how you managed to survive your body for so long, and the mermaid is right. You memorize the face you woke up to every morning since you could live with the mermaid, hold onto it, and you let go.

❧

The sound of hovering helicopters startles you awake in the swamp of the boy who coughs up oil's body. You ask the swamp what's going on, and it doesn't answer. Sunlight starts entering the swamp more and more, and you feel something burrowing towards you. You try to swim away, but you can't. The swamp locked your body in place. The burrowing stops and the swamp collapses and you fall down. You get up and see guards and tanks surrounding you. You put your hands up, look around, and see your best friend, and the boy who oozes with their hands up. You're surprised the guards haven't shot either of you being that all of you were in a quarantine zone, being that all of you should have been cauterized by whatever the American god directs the government to use to burn disease out of buildings, out of countries. The guards drop their guns and kneel and pray. Everyone in the tanks gets out; kneels; prays. The helicopters fly away. You ask: *what's going on,* and one of the guards says: *you three are the first to survive a cauterization. The American god has deemed you holy.* You get on your knees to pretend to thank the American god for his blessing, and your best friend, and the boy who oozes do the same. You bow your head so no one can see you smiling how for the first time ever, the idea of an American god saved you.

100

The first thing your best friend did during the first televised interview with you, her, and the boy who oozes about your miraculous survival was come out and admit she loved other girls in the way girls are supposed to love boys, and the studio audience leaned back in horror at this revelation, started murmuring amongst each other that it wasn't possible that the American god would spare someone who betrays the values he protects with his golden AK-47, and your best friend could tell they questioned their faith, the American god's judgement so she stood up and said: *how can I be a monster when the American god made me this way?* The studio became so quiet, all you could hear was the camera lenses focusing in and out, and then someone started applauding and the applause infected the crowd. The moment you and her were alone, you asked her why she took that risk, and she said: *I want the love that you could have had, even if it doesn't last. I'm willing to die for it.* When someone tried to kill her outside of the studio, the crowd around you and her and the boy who oozes pulled out their guns and executed the would-be assassin. Their bullets sent this message to everyone: love who you want and if you try to stop that love, the American god gives us permission to cure you of your existence.

The first thing you did after you settled in your new home was break into the boy who coughs up oil's house and rescue his collection of cassette tapes before the government turned his house into a shrine. You picked a tape to listen to every night to lull you to sleep, to have the dates you would have had with the boy who coughs up oil if he were still alive in your dreams. Even in those dreams, the furthest you go with him is second base. You had to fill in the gaps of what his touch felt like with the touch of the other boys you ever kissed or touched, sometimes having to put his face and his cough on another boy's body. You did this for a year and as the year went by, you broke up and got back together and broke up and got back together and broke up and got back together until the boy who coughs up oil became an apparition of his wants. The last tape you listened to said *I'll never lose this pain/Never dream of you again*, and you used to cry when you heard those lyrics, but you don't anymore. You shelved the tapes and the grief.

You ran into the boy (now a man) who oozes five years after the miracle in a supermarket. Initially, the three of you were shuffled from place to place questioned about the miracle, then trotted out around the country as proof of the American god's benevolence. After the government finally left all of you alone, the boy who oozes decided to help those that he would have used as bricks in the wall he wanted to build around heaven, his way for atoning for all the awful things he's done, his way of showing the boy who coughs up oil that he was worthy of saving. You almost didn't recognize him and almost wouldn't have said anything to him until he called your name, and you looked at him. He asked you to dinner, and you said yes, without hesitation. Over wine (water for you since you quit drinking after the miracle, since you no longer needed to escape your mother under the ocean of your feelings), you catch up and when he reached for your hand, you let him hold it, let him take you home, let him in your bed; he hasn't left your side since.

On the fifteenth anniversary of the miracle, you, your husband, your daughter (the girl with a boy's name), your best friend, and her partner make an appearance at the cauterization site. You are here to say hello to your constituents as the first congresswoman in any district in the last 50 years. The government erected a fence around the blast site to keep the ruins, to remind people what happens when illness grows out of control, how the American god can save you when you least expect it. Your daughter tugs at your pants leg, asks, *is that where you got my name from*, and you say: yes. *If it wasn't for him, you wouldn't be here today.*

She asks what the boy who coughs up oil was like, and you say: *brave,
like you.* You swear you hear the boy who coughs up oil use the wind to
say how much he misses you, and you nod and think about how much
you miss him, too.

Acknowledgements

This book was written to the following music;
- *Dirty Projectors* – Dirty Projectors
- *Carrie & Lowell Live* – Sufjan Stevens
- "The System Dreams In Total Darkness" – The National

Parts of this book have appeared in *Lost Balloon*, *Drunk In A Midnight Choir*, *Hot Tub Astronaut*, and *Dash Literary Journal*.

Special thanks to everyone who followed along on my Instagram feed as I was writing this novel.

About the Author

J. Bradley lives at jbradleywrites.com.

About the Publisher

Whisk(e)y Tit is committed to restoring degradation and degeneracy to the literary arts. We work with authors who are unwilling to sacrifice intellectual rigor, unrelenting playfulness, and visual beauty in our literary pursuits, often leading to texts that would otherwise be abandoned in today's largely homogenized literary landscape. In a world governed by idiocy, our commitment to these principles is an act of civil service and civil disobedience alike.